The guy wit 12-04 **DATE DUE** zard,"
he cried, jab

Not that again. "Leave me alone. It's just a game!"
Maybe they came from one of those countries that was
stuck in the Dark Ages—a place where angry mobs killed
anyone they thought was practicing magic. I dropped my
hands and took a step back, scanning the walls on either
side for any way out. As my right hand brushed my jacket,
I got a wild idea.

"Make us," Hurko said.

"Okay, I'll make you," I said. "This will teach you not to
mess with a wizard." I grabbed the flash ball I'd gotten
from Jenna. With luck, the surprise would give me time to
escape. I wanted to shout something that sounded like a
magic word. But all my frozen brain could come up with
was, "*¡Albóndigas!*"

Hoping that none of them spoke Spanish well enough
to realize I'd just shouted, "Meatballs," I closed my eyes
against the flash and threw the ball to the ground between
me and Hurko.

"The plot will keep readers turning the pages. . . . A fun, quick
read; a good choice for reluctant readers."   *—KLIATT*

"Breezy and funny."   *—Booklist*

"The story combines wizardry and the real world of eighth
grade in a way that is entirely believable and thought-
provoking."   *—School Library Journal*

OTHER BOOKS YOU MAY ENJOY

Wizards

of the

Game

David Lubar

PUFFIN BOOKS

Many thanks to Sally Keehn,
who introduced me to Nancy Springer,
who introduced me to Michael Green,
who introduced me to Mercer and the Wizards.

PUFFIN BOOKS
Published by Penguin Group
Penguin Young Readers Group,
345 Hudson Street, New York, New York 10014, U.S.A.
Penguin Books Ltd, 80 Strand, London WC2R ORL, England
Penguin Books Australia Ltd, 250 Camberwell Road, Camberwell, Victoria 3124, Australia
Penguin Books Canada Ltd, 10 Alcorn Avenue, Toronto, Ontario, Canada M4V 3B2
Penguin Group (NZ), cnr Airborne and Rosedale Roads, Albany, Auckland 1310, New Zealand

First published in the United States of America by Philomel Books,
a division of Penguin Putnam Books for Young Readers, 2003
Published by Puffin Books, a division of Penguin Young Readers Group, 2004

1 3 5 7 9 10 8 6 4 2

THE LIBRARY OF CONGRESS HAS CATALOGED THE PHILOMEL EDITION AS FOLLOWS:
Lubar, David.
Wizards of the game / David Lubar.
p.   cm.
Summary: Eighth grader Mercer, whose passion is the fantasy role-playing game
Wizards of the Warrior World, hopes to use a fund-raiser to bring a gaming
convention to his middle school, but instead he attracts four genuine wizards
who are trapped on Earth and want his help in returning to their own world.
ISBN: 0-399-23706-2 (hc)
[1. Fantasy games—Fiction. 2. Magic—Fiction. 3. Wizards—Fiction.
4. Schools—Fiction.] I. Title.
PZ7.L96775 Wi 2003
[Fic]—dc21 2002003640

Puffin Books ISBN 0-14-240215-X
Designed by Gina DiMassi. Text set in Century Expanded.

Printed in the United States of America

For my talented friend
Dian Curtis Regan
who was kind to me
even when we were strangers.

Table of Contents

1

Killing Time

Shortly, if the ancient maps were correct, I'd face my sworn enemy. Soon, I'd discover whether the sword of Calandra was a magical weapon capable of defeating an army, or a worthless piece of iron I'd been tricked into buying through the clever promises of a lying wizard. Not much longer, I told myself, trying to control the excitement that buzzed through my nerves with the energy of a thousand wasps. Soon, revenge would be mine. Soon, the head of Maraku would dangle from my belt, and his heart would nourish the wolves who followed my trail.

But first, I had to make it through the rest of my third-period geography class.

I glanced at the clock again while Mr. Abruzzi described the many natural resources of Central America. Sixteen minutes to go. Less than a thousand seconds.

Over to my left, Kyle Tate, who was one of my gaming buddies, grinned at me and whispered, "Hang in there." He flashed the Palm of Power, a secret hand signal used only among members of the Warrior-Mage clan.

"Can't wait," I whispered back.

Fifteen minutes.

For that dragging stretch of time, I'd have to sit in my seat in the third row of room 298 and be Mercer Dickensen, earthbound eighth-grade student at Oscar Wilde Middle School. But then, for all of free period, I'd be Shath'dra, sixth-level Warrior-Mage, fighting to survive and gain wealth and power in the treacherous world of Zule.

Wizards of the Warrior World. That was our game. We sought adventure in a land of spells and swordplay.

Fourteen minutes.

"Major exports of Panama?" Mr. Abruzzi asked me, slipping up to my desk from the right as I checked the clock above the door on my left.

"Bananas, pineapples, and copper," I answered instantly, taking him by surprise. The real world was a battleground, too. I'd just dodged a spear thrust and countered with a deadly triple slash.

"Right, Mercer," Mr. Abruzzi said. "Very good." He turned from me, I guess in search of weaker foes.

Actually, I enjoyed geography, but it was hard to keep my mind in the real world when there were richer realms to explore. And enemies to fight. The streets of town paled before the dirt paths of Zule.

When Mr. Abruzzi returned to the front of the room, Ed "the Head" Bingham glanced over his shoulder and said, "Want to go to the library next period? We can work on our assignment."

"Can't," I said. Ed and I had to do a project for English. Ms. Reuter had paired us up randomly. I didn't know much about Ed, but he seemed pretty smart. He worked on the school paper, so I figured he knew how to write. Last time, I'd been teamed with Dooley Cronk, who held the school record for fastest consumption of a bowl of cafeteria Jell-O. Two point seven seconds. I wouldn't have believed it if I hadn't been there. Unfortunately, Dooley's awesome skills at sucking up Jell-O were balanced by an equally extreme inability to spit out a single solid sentence. I'd ended up doing the report myself.

After getting stuck with Dooley, I sure didn't mind being paired with Ed. The problem was finding time to work together. This weekend was out. There was a marathon gaming session at the Comic Nook. Noon to seven on Saturday and noon to five on Sunday. No way I was going to miss that.

"We need to get started," Ed said. "It's an important paper—ten percent of our grade. We can't mess around. College is less than five years away." His gaze flicked toward the front of the room, where Mr. Abruzzi was writing on the board, then back to me. "You sure you can't make it to the library? I thought you had study hall next period."

"I'm busy. How about later?" I asked.

"*Later* is what my dad says when he doesn't want to do something." Ed sighed and shifted his eyes away from me. "Look, if you're that busy, don't worry about it. I can get started on my own. It's not a problem. I usually end up doing all the writing, anyhow."

Good grief. I hadn't been trying to brush him off. "How about after school?" I asked.

"Sounds good," Ed said. "I'm free. I'll meet you out front."

I nodded and glanced at the clock. All right—six more minutes had slipped by. Eight to go.

My mind drifted for a while, playing out the upcoming battle in various ways. In each version, I achieved total victory.

Three minutes to go.

Two.

One.

I had my books in my hand, my butt off my seat, and my feet on the floor the instant the clock ticked past that final minute. By the time the bell kicked in, I was halfway down the aisle.

"Eddy and Michelle," Mr. Abruzzi called over the noise

of the class's flight toward the door, "I'd like to see you for a moment."

Tough luck, I thought as Ed and Michelle stopped dead in their tracks. I moved through the crowd that was funneling out, ready to join the flowing mobs in the hall and make my way as quickly as possible downstairs to room 157. It was finally game time. I felt like a parched man crawling through a desert toward a vat of vanilla milk shakes. Watch out, Maraku, here I come. Feel my sword. Taste my vengeance. Eat cold metal.

"And you, too, Mercer," Mr. Abruzzi said just before I reached the hallway. "Could I see you for a moment, please."

2

Raising Trouble

If I'd been braver, I'd have pretended I didn't hear Mr. Abruzzi call my name. But when I thought about ducking into the hall, I felt this tiny tingle deep in my gut. I guess it's like those electric collars that keep dogs on the lawn.

I turned and walked to the front of the class. By now, I figured everyone else was headed for room 157. In a couple minutes, they'd be setting up the game, spreading the maps, and rolling the dice. Those weasels would start without me. The truth is, if I were in their place, I'd do the same thing.

Meanwhile, Ed, obviously eager to please anyone capable of giving him a good grade, was hovering millimeters from the left corner of Mr. Abruzzi's desk. Michelle Titlebaum, cool as always, with a face so pretty it could make your heart hurt to think about it for too long, stood calmly near the right side of the desk. I joined them in the middle, keeping an equal distance from the two extremes of the popularity spectrum.

"Why did you want to see us, Mr. Abruzzi?" Ed asked before the teacher could say a word.

"You all know about the fire at Zampala Chocolates?" he asked.

"Sure," I said. The pictures from the TV news report flashed through my mind. The place had burned to the ground last month after the night watchman fell asleep with a cigar in his hand and a half-eaten jumbo box of chocolate-covered cherries in his lap. Big news in a small town like this. I'll never forget how great the air smelled for days afterward.

"Normally, the eighth grade sells Zampala chocolate bars to raise money for our Kids Kare program," Mr. Abruzzi said. "We could switch brands, but at the staff meeting yesterday we decided it would be good to give the students a chance to suggest some ideas. You three are among the more creative members of this class, so I figured I'd see what you could dream up."

He paused, and you could hear each of us thinking in the silence. I didn't know what the others had in mind, but I was wondering whether Mr. Abruzzi was done with us for the moment.

"Can we take our time?" Michelle asked.

Thank you, I thought. Maybe we wouldn't be stuck here for the whole period discussing the eternal question of whether a car wash was more profitable than a sandwich sale. If I hurried, I could still get downstairs before the game started.

"Sure," Mr. Abruzzi said. "Good idea, Michelle. Take a little time. Give it some thought. Maybe we can kick around your ideas on Monday. But we can't wait too long. School's over in less than two months."

"Sounds great," I said, taking a step backward. "Monday." I took another step.

"Mr. Abruzzi?" Ed asked. For some reason—I guess just out of habit—he raised his hand.

"Yes, Ed?"

"Do you want us to work as a team?" Ed's eyes shot over toward Michelle for a microsecond, then bounced away as if they'd rolled against a hot stove.

Shut up, Ed, I thought, trying to will him to develop laryngitis.

"That's for you three to decide," Mr. Abruzzi said.

"Monday," I repeated. "Let's discuss it then." I managed one more backward step with each word.

"Wait, I have a great idea," Ed said. He raised his hand again.

My next three words were going to be, "Well, see ya," but I never got the chance. On the first step, I tripped over a desk. My feet stopped dead, but the rest of me kept going. I twisted, stumbled, and lost my balance. For a brief instant, I almost recovered, but I ended up rolling over the desk with a move that would have been worth major points in any Olympic gymnastics competition. Except for the dismount. I blew that big time. They don't give a high score for landing on your back. As my books rained down around me, Mr. Abruzzi rushed over.

"Good heavens, Mercer, are you all right?" he asked.

"I'm fine." I climbed to my feet, ignoring the various pains that shot through the impact area, and avoiding the urge to check out Michelle's reaction. I really didn't want to see her face right then.

"Maybe you should go to the nurse," Mr. Abruzzi said.

"Really, I'm fine. See you all on Monday." I scooped up my books and dashed toward the door.

Behind me, I heard Ed saying, "It's an awesome idea. Totally cool. Anyone want to hear it?"

I reached the hall and sprinted full out, hoping I wouldn't get snagged by one of the handful of teachers who lived for no greater pleasure than to yell at kids like me. As I turned the corner, someone shouted, "Wet floor."

Wet *and* slippery.

Donny, the janitor, yanked his mop out of my path as I slid by. This time, I managed to keep my balance.

I slowed for a second to glance back at him. "Sorry."

"No problem." He spun his mop around, almost like it was a weapon, and went back to swabbing the floor.

I took the stairs four at a time, using the railing to make the turn at the landing the way a space probe uses the sun as a sling to build velocity. A final leap and I cleared the last eight steps.

All right. Through the door and up the hall. Room 157. I stepped inside, trying to catch my breath.

"There you are," Kyle said as I reached our table.

"Here I am." I pulled out my chair, eager for battle.

The room had four long tables, each with six seats. A half dozen pairs of kids sat at smaller tables. They played a short version that just used cards. But we liked the long version, which was a role-playing game, complete with maps and a Game Lord who controlled the action. A good campaign could last for weeks, or even months.

Ms. Sebastian, who taught algebra, was on duty today. Believe it or not, teachers fought for a turn to be here. It beat getting stuck in one of the regular study halls. We were too busy casting spells and slaying monsters to cause any trouble.

I grabbed my equipment from my backpack. Cards, dice, spell book, maps, notes, and a hand-painted metal figure of Shath'dra.

"Hey, Mercer," Drew Unger said, greeting me from his seat across the table. He reached down and adjusted the figure of Maraku that stood in front of him.

"Hey, Drew." I nodded, trying not to give any hint that I was about to unleash my sword and slice him up like a birthday cake.

3

Stripped of All Dignity

It was an incredibly brief battle. The sword, after all I'd gone through to obtain it, might just as well have been made of cheese. I barely escaped with my life. Dying sucks, because you don't get to choose how you come back. It's all based on fate. You have to roll five dice and check the reincarnation table. The way my luck was running, I'd have gotten stuck playing the rest of the campaign as a camel herder or a tavern maid.

To make my defeat even worse, Maraku smacked me with a level-nine flameblaster spell. My defense roll came up with such low numbers that the fire burned everything I owned, including my clothing.

As I waited for my next turn after fleeing to the safety of the Manthrigian Wasteland, I glared at Lytheria, who'd sold me the sword. She grinned at me and shrugged.

We had a rule—keep it in the game. No matter what anyone did to you, it stayed in the world of Zule. Right now, Lytheria could gloat over my defeat. Once the bell rang, sending Shath'dra, Lytheria, Maraku, and the others into that timeless realm where adventurers dwelled between games, I knew Jenna Vanderbeek—as she was called in the mortal world—would lose the grin. But during the session, which I spent trying to scrounge up clothing and a weapon, such thoughts did little to improve my mood.

We played until the period ended. Then I hustled to put my stuff away.

"No hard feelings?" Jenna asked, giving me a playful punch on the shoulder. She'd become a real pain ever since she started taking those karate classes last year. But I'd known her so long, I was used to her being one kind of pain or another.

"No hard feelings," I said, making an effort to sound like a good sport. I'm not sure I succeeded.

I spent the rest of the school day replaying my defeat and trying to imagine any possible way the battle could have worked out differently. No matter how many times I ran the scene through my head, I always ended up butt-naked and in full retreat.

For variety, I reran the tumbling act I'd performed in front of Michelle. As much as I tried to create a version where I landed triumphantly on my feet, it never came out that way.

By the time my last class had ended, I was eager to get home. I needed to go through my strategy books and work out a plan to recover everything I'd lost. I rushed to my locker, and then headed for the door.

"Ready?" Ed's voice broke through my thoughts as I reached the bottom of the front steps.

"For what?"

"Our project," he said.

"Oh yeah. Sure." I tried to act like I hadn't forgotten, but he wasn't fooled.

"Look, I really don't mind doing it myself. I'm used to working alone. It's no problem."

Now I felt rotten again. "No, I want to do this with you. You're right—it's important. Okay?"

I guess he really had to think about it because he sighed twice before he finally said, "Okay."

As we walked toward my house, we discussed the project. It wasn't a hard one. We just had to pick two or three characters from classic books and put them into an original piece of writing set in modern times. The project could take any form we wanted—a play, a story, a movie script. Ms. Reuter was flexible.

"Shakespeare's pretty cool," I said. I'd seen some movies of his plays. "We could use the witches from *Macbeth*. You know, the ones stirring the big pot. We could put them in a soup commercial. Or a cooking show." I waited for Ed to tell me how much he loved the idea.

"I'd rather stay away from witches," he said.

That was a drag, but I guess he was right. When I tried to make my projects too radical, I ended up getting a bad grade. Some teachers weren't big fans of fantasy. That didn't make sense, because there's nothing like fantasy to stretch your mind.

"Here's my house," I told Ed when we reached the end of Dewberry Street. "You like games?" I asked as I headed up the porch and opened the front door.

"Sure," he said. "Why?"

"Just wondering." I grinned at the thought of showing Ed my room. It was a game player's heaven—a shrine to other realms. I couldn't wait to see his reaction.

"I'm home," I shouted down the hall. Mom shouted something back. The smell of fresh-baked bread made my stomach rumble. Bread is Mom's hobby. Actually, she calls it her *therapy*. She bakes whenever she begins working on a new job. She's a freelance interior designer. She helps companies pick out furniture, rugs, curtains, and even the paintings for the walls. Dad and I encouraged her to take new jobs all the time, since the bread is generally amazing.

"This way." I climbed the stairs and turned left toward my room. "Behold," I said, pushing the door open and stepping inside. I wanted to go first so I could get a good look at Ed's expression.

"Thanks." Ed followed me in, then froze. My room has that effect on everybody. I'd turned it into Zule, complete with the twin suns Helimis and Solimis painted high on one wall above the barren Kallus Mountains and the deadly Desert of Lost Hopes. I also had posters of all the demigods who fought to control the mortals, a half dozen small sculptures of various Zulean creatures, and a full-sized statue of a lava demon that I'd made in art class. Even crouched over, the demon's curved horns nearly brushed the ceiling.

"Cool, huh?" I asked Ed.

As the silence grew longer, I realized he didn't look amazed, impressed, or blown away. Not at all. Instead, he looked like someone who'd just come face-to-face with a really bad traffic accident.

4

A Devil of a Problem

Ed shuffled backward, glanced at me, then stared at the lava demon again. "Are you some kind of devil worshipper?" he asked.

"What?" I wasn't sure how to answer such a ridiculous question, so I laughed. But the sound died against the walls. "This?" I asked, pointing to the statue. "Is this what you're talking about?"

Ed nodded.

"I made it in art class last month," I told him. I guess Ed had never seen it before because he had band practice instead of art. "It's not a devil. It's newspaper and paste."

"It's got horns and a tail," Ed said.

So does a bull, I thought. But I figured this wasn't a good time to be a wise guy. "Sure, it's called a lava demon, but that's not like a real devil. It's just a name. It doesn't mean anything. A horsefly isn't a horse, right? And what about deviled eggs? None of this is anything bad."

"Why do you have it?" Ed asked.

I waved my hand around the room. "Everything's from the game—Wizards of the Warrior World. Those are forest angels," I said, pointing to a poster next to my closet. I figured a pair of angels should more than make up for one demon. Especially angels who looked like supermodels.

"It's a game?" Ed asked.

I nodded. "Sure. That's all."

"But you're fooling around with demons," Ed said. "My church warns against that."

This wasn't getting us anywhere. "Look, if it bothers you, we can work in another room."

He scanned the walls again, then nodded. "Yeah, if you don't mind."

"We can use the kitchen," I said as I headed downstairs. "It's a demon-free zone." I grinned over my shoulder at Ed. He didn't return my smile. I still couldn't believe he was serious.

We sat at the table and discussed the project. Ed started to relax a bit, but I could tell he wasn't completely comfortable, mostly because he didn't talk as much as usual. We came up with a couple ideas, but nothing we both liked.

"Want to meet again tomorrow afternoon?" Ed asked after he'd put away his notes.

"I can't." I ran the gaming schedule through my mind,

looking for an open time. "How about I call you Sunday morning? I'm free until just before noon."

He shook his head. "I'll be at church."

"Maybe your folks will let you skip it if you tell them you have a school project," I said.

"I don't want to skip it," Ed said. "I like church. What about Sunday evening?"

That would work. I'd be back from the Comic Nook by early evening. "Sounds fine." I got up from the table, but Ed stayed seated.

"Want to talk about the fund-raiser?" he asked.

I checked the clock on the microwave. My gamer's chat started in ten minutes. We met online every Friday. But I knew Ed was dying to tell me his idea. "Yeah, we can kick things around for a bit."

"Great. Wait a second. Maybe it's not fair for us to discuss it without Michelle. I'd hate for her to think we went behind her back or anything."

"Don't worry. I'm sure she won't feel left out." I figured the last thing Michelle would want is an invitation to hang around with Ed and me.

"I guess you're right." Ed sighed and stuck his pen back in his shirt pocket. "She's probably never felt left out in her whole life."

"Probably not."

"Anyhow, here's what I was thinking. My church has a bake sale every year. They raise a ton of money. I figured we could hold some sort of sale at the school. Not just cakes and cookies, either. We could sell lots of things—books, clothes, furniture. Kind of a neighborhood garage sale, except the garage is the school gym. People can donate stuff for us to sell. Or they can pay for a spot and sell their own stuff. Either way, we'd make money."

"Hey, that's not a bad idea," I said. "I like it."

"So, if I bring it up at the meeting, can I count on your vote?"

"Unless Michelle has an idea," I said. "No way I'm voting against her, even if she suggests we dress up in hula skirts and dance on our hands in a pool of raw sewage."

"Oh." Ed's eyes shifted toward the floor, and his body seemed to deflate slightly.

"Relax. That was just a joke. I look terrible in a hula skirt. And I think I'm allergic to sewage. Last time they served it in the cafeteria, I broke out in a rash. Listen, your idea's great. I'm sure Mr. Abruzzi will love it."

"You think so?" Ed asked.

"Absolutely."

"Thanks. Well, I'd better get home. I have to start working on my next column for the school paper. It's due Tuesday morning." Ed stood up and headed toward the door.

"Hey," I said as I followed him down the hall.

"What?"

"This is all harmless." I pointed back toward my room. "Honest. I don't hide up there killing chickens or sticking pins in dolls. It's just a game. Some kids fill their walls with pictures of professional wrestlers. Now *that's* spooky."

"Yeah. I guess." Ed didn't look very convinced.

I took another shot at proving I wasn't Satan's younger brother. "You know, this has nothing to do with religion."

"Maybe that's the problem." Ed stepped onto the porch. "I'll call you Sunday after dinner."

"I'll talk to you then."

"You won't forget, will you?" he asked.

"Of course not," I said. And I actually believed I was telling the truth.

5

The Downside of Downtown

Five o'clock. Chat time. Upstairs, as I waited for the modem to dial in, I tried to make sense out of Ed's reaction to my room. I didn't get it. There was nothing wrong with anything I was doing. I didn't listen to weird music. I didn't act like death was cool or life was meaningless. I didn't own a Ouija board and tarot cards like Jenna. And I certainly didn't hurt anybody. I just enjoyed fantasy. I loved games. That's all.

I wondered what Michelle would have said. She'd probably think I was weird. My world revolved around magic swords and secret spells. Hers was built on field hockey sticks and shopping malls. But we had one thing in common—we were both awesome in our chosen world.

I heard various clicks as my PC finished logging in. The chat room was packed. A couple of the guys were excited about a gaming convention in their city this weekend. They promised to give a full report next Friday.

I'd love to go to a convention. They have dealers, demonstrations, swap meets, guest speakers, art shows, and all kinds of stuff. Some people even wear costumes. It sounded like a total blast. But there'd never been a convention anywhere near here.

At six, when the chat ended, my little sister Tracy dashed into my room. "Mom said to tell you dinner's in five minutes."

"Be right there," I told her as she skipped back out to the hallway. I logged off and went downstairs.

Dad was just getting home from work. He's a programmer for an insurance company. Mom was slicing a fresh loaf of Italian bread. A pot of spaghetti sauce bubbled on top of the stove. It smelled so good, I almost drooled.

"What's new?" Dad asked after we'd all sat down.

"Not much. Got an 89 on my math quiz. Hit a double in gym. Learned to use a table saw in shop class." I wiggled my fingers to show I hadn't lost any. "And I'm helping with the Kids Kare fund-raiser."

"Good for you," Dad said.

"There's a new book coming out on water spells," I added. No point letting a *good-for-you* go to waste.

"You just got new sneakers," Dad said.

"That doesn't count," I said. "I *needed* sneakers."

"Don't you have a whole shelf of spell books already?" Mom asked.

"Not one that's just for water spells. This book has everything."

Mom and Dad nodded, which meant I had a pretty good shot at getting the book. There were a couple other things I needed, but I figured I should spread out my requests.

Tracy took over and gave a much longer account of her day. We could usually make it all the way to dessert before she ran out of details. Which was fine. I was happy to eat and let someone else talk.

After dinner, and a bit of television, I went to my room and studied my strategy guides. I didn't plan to take another thumping like the one I'd just received. No way I was getting chased by any more wizards.

When I got into bed, I stared past my feet at the lava demon. I guess he might seem a little spooky if you didn't know better. Especially if you met him unexpectedly.

"Behave yourself," I said to him as I turned off the light.

I took care of all my weekend chores Saturday morning, then finished my homework. By eleven-thirty, I was ready to head out for the Comic Nook. As I grabbed my jacket from the hall closet, Mom came over to me, along with Tracy.

"Mercer, I need a favor," she said.

"I'm leaving," I said. "My game's about to start."

"Perfect. Tracy is supposed to go to Kendra's. I don't have time to drive her. Can you walk her there?" Mom asked.

"I'll be late," I said, picturing my sister's less-than-rapid walking speed and her ability to come to a dead halt at the slightest distraction.

"No you won't," Mom said. "It's right on your way."

I realized if I spent time trying to talk her out of it, I'd definitely be late. "Hurry up," I told Tracy. "Get your coat."

I rushed Tracy out the door and down Dewberry Street. Our house is only a couple blocks from the main shopping section on Broad Street. The Comic Nook is six blocks south of there, at the corner of Broad and Hastings.

Broad Street is kind of a mixed area. There are a lot of new shops, but some of the old places have gone out of business. There's a two-block stretch where nearly all the stores are boarded up. The funny thing is, the next block is a lot nicer. And the block after that, where Tracy's friend lives, is just fine. It's like the town is growing but little bits of it are dying at the same time.

In the middle of the second block of the bad part, between an abandoned minimart and an empty furniture store, we walked past the Sharing Shepherd. The building used to be a clothing store. The old name was still painted on the front window in chipped gold letters—Mr. Buck's Tuxes and Ties. No tuxedos these days. Now it's a shelter.

There were about a dozen men and women on the sidewalk near the door, drinking coffee from Styrofoam cups. Another smaller group had gathered off to the side. Through the window, I saw more people sitting at tables and on a couple couches. I just took a quick glance because I didn't want anyone to think I was staring. As we walked by, Tracy waved and said, "Hi."

I groaned. This was no time—or place—for her to be making new friends. Several people waved back, but most of them ignored us.

"Pretty girl," an old woman with a scarf tied around her head said, smiling at Tracy.

"You're pretty, too. I'm going to see Kendra. My brother's walking me there," Tracy added, pointing to me. Her voice got louder with each sentence. "He's going to go cast spells and fight monsters. He's a wizard. He's got a million books full of spells."

"Come *on*," I said, taking her hand. The place spooked me. Mom's explained that the people in the shelter aren't any different from everyone else—just down on their luck. But when I got close to them, it felt like they were from another world—a world I knew nothing about.

As we walked toward the corner, I heard a shout from behind. It sounded like, "Make us!" but that made no sense. Make us do what?

I glanced over my shoulder. A man in the smaller group was waving his fist at me. He was short, maybe just an inch or two taller than I was, with a dark, droopy mustache that made him look like a thin walrus. He wore an old army coat, red corduroy pants, and a beat-up black cowboy hat. "Make us!" he shouted again. I still had no idea what he was screaming about. For an instant, our eyes locked. There was something wild and desperate in his gaze. I sped away, half dragging Tracy.

"What's wrong?" she asked.

"Don't want to be late," I said, trying to sound calm. I managed to keep my voice steady, but deep inside, I shivered.

6

Let the Games Begin

The Comic Nook was mobbed. A couple months ago, the owners had cleared a space at the back of the store and set up a table for gamers to use on the weekends. It was a good move. The players bought lots of supplies. As the game got more popular, the owners added a second table, and then a third. This weekend, there were seven tables, and that was barely enough.

"Big crowd," I said to one of the owners as I walked past the counter.

"Yup. It just keeps growing."

"Maybe you should run a tournament," I said.

He shrugged. "I'd love to. Not enough space. I'd bet a couple hundred players would show up."

"Wow. That many?" It would be awesome to be surrounded by a mob of game fans.

"Definitely. This crowd's local. They'd come from all over for a tournament. I'm sure of it. Speaking of crowds, you'd better grab a spot before they're all gone."

"Good idea." I snaked my way through the store and plunked down at one of the tables. Someone else filled the last seat and we got started.

"You are in the ruins of Nazother, an abandoned city near the Valley of Slaughter," the Game Lord said, reading from the open booklet in front of him.

That's how a game starts. The Game Lord uses a booklet that described our situation. It's called a *scenario*. They sold them at the Comic Nook. The scenario had details on hidden treasures, traps, monsters, and all sorts of cool stuff.

Each player took the role of a character he'd created. I usually became Shath'dra, though I had several other characters I'd play on occasion. For each new game, Shath'dra had to start from scratch, with nothing more than a small ration of food and a handful of money. Players received a limited number of points—determined by a roll of the dice—to divide among traits such as power, magic, wisdom, luck, and intuition. The more points, the stronger that ability.

Players also got to select their heritage. Every character was a mix of wizard, warrior, thief, diplomat, hero, and dozens of other bloodlines. The combinations were endless. A player could even have monsters and demigods among his ancestors, though there were always weaknesses to balance strengths, so nobody started with an unfair advantage.

"Tell me your name," the Game Lord said, looking to his left.

One by one, moving clockwise, we spoke the names of our adventurers. Then we each handed the Game Lord a list with information about our character. The lists were kept secret. Only the Game Lord knew, for instance, that Shath'dra was able to heal instantly from any wound caused by a bronze weapon. Or that he could cast certain powerful spells during the last hour of the day. Those abilities had cost me weaknesses in other areas, but I figured they'd prove useful.

On my first turn, I was immediately ambushed.

"Three trolls lumber toward you from behind the fallen walls of a shrine, shaking the very ground as they bellow inhuman howls of rage," the Game Lord said. "The stench alone would drop a weaker warrior."

"I attack the one in front," I said, rolling the battle dice. Luckily, I'd loaded up on agility and speed. Trolls were powerful, but they were also slow.

The Game Lord rolled the defense dice for the troll and checked the combat resolution table. "You deal your adversary a crippling blow with your short sword." Another roll, using a pair of twelve-sided dice, produced more results. "He falls with a thunderous crash, dropping a pouch containing seven gleaming gold coins and a glowing gem of a kind you've never seen before."

The Game Lord turned to the next player. "The road you have chosen splits. The right fork rises toward a cemetery. The left fork curves past a large stone statue that toppled on its side and shattered many centuries ago. The face of the statue is crushed and indistinguishable. What do you do?"

I'd have to wait for my next turn to continue my fight with the trolls. I didn't mind. This Game Lord was good, which made the game even more fun.

A crowd of spectators circled our table—mostly younger kids who probably wanted to learn the game before playing. One of them tapped my shoulder and whispered, "What kind of gem did you get?"

"I don't know. I'll have to figure it out." I turned to listen to the Game Lord as he described the encounter between the player two seats to my right and a mysterious, ghostly figure.

And so it went for the rest of the afternoon, while we lived through a full week of adventures on Zule. I had a great time, especially when another player attacked me with a bronze javelin. He was pretty surprised by my healing power. Even better, the attack came during the last hour of the day, so I could use special magic. I blew the poor sucker away with a smithereen spell.

I went back on Sunday. The second session was just as much fun, even when the glowing gem turned out to be a fake that struck me with an itching spell. It's hard to swing a sword when you need both hands for scratching. But I ended the campaign with a pile of treasure and a ton of experience points. Everyone in the place had a good time. The young kids seemed to enjoy watching the game just as much as the players enjoyed playing it.

On the way home from the Comic Nook, I crossed the street to avoid the Sharing Shepherd. A couple people were hanging around in front, but I didn't see the guy who'd shouted at me.

It had been a great weekend, but I had to go back to school tomorrow. Back to classes and tests. That was okay. I figured the fund-raising stuff would be fun. Not as much fun as a gaming convention, but it would be okay. . . .

And that's when everything clicked together in my mind. I froze for a second, stunned by the perfect way it all worked out, then rushed home. The moment I got inside, I ran to my room so I could go online and hunt down the information I needed. This was definitely the coolest idea I'd ever had. I couldn't wait to share it.

7

Meeting With Some Problems

I stayed on the computer until I got booted off. Not by a power surge, but the old-fashioned way—by Mom pointing out it was time for bed.

"You have school tomorrow," she reminded me, as if there was a kid on the planet who didn't know when Monday was about to pounce. You could almost feel it creeping around the globe on Sunday evening, devouring Europe and then swimming eagerly west.

I gathered up my notes, grabbed the stuff I'd printed out, jammed everything in a folder, and glanced at the clock. Man, it was late. The Net could really eat up the hours. I was beat, but I was excited, too, and that made it hard for me to fall asleep. So I kept my light on and studied one of my strategy guides until I drifted off.

In the morning, as I walked to school, I examined my

idea for any weak points. As far as I could see, it was perfect. I'd tried to come up with answers for every possible objection. It reminded me of getting ready for battle against a high-level wizard. I was prepared to counter any spell that was tossed at me. If I pulled it off, I'd be a hero with my gaming buddies. This seemed like one of those rare times when everybody would win.

My first-period science class crawled by. So did gym class. The moment I reached geography, I dropped my books on my desk, then grabbed the folder with the papers and rushed over to Mr. Abruzzi. "When can we tell you our ideas?" As the words tumbled from my mouth, I had a sudden fear that I was turning into Ed.

"I don't see why we can't have a quick discussion right now. We can use the meeting room." He waited for the rest of the students to trickle in, then said, "Class, start reading chapter nineteen. I'll be back shortly. Michelle, Ed, please come with Mercer and me."

I wasn't sure whether teachers were supposed to leave a class alone, but they did it all the time and nobody minded. It gave the teachers a break, and it gave the students a break. And, usually, nothing beyond the rules got broken. Behind us, as the door closed, I could almost hear the first paper airplane swooshing through the air. I didn't think anyone was about to make much of a dent in chapter nineteen.

"What happened?" Ed asked as we walked toward the meeting room.

"What do you mean?"

"We were supposed to talk last night, right? Our English project. Sound familiar? I tried to call you for hours, but the line was busy."

"Oh man, I'm sorry." I'd been so caught up in my idea, I'd forgotten all about our project. And I'd stayed online the whole evening, so the phone was busy. Mom had a separate line for business, but I hadn't thought to give Ed that number. "I got tied up with some stuff. Are you free after school?"

"Are *you*?" he asked.

"Yeah. I am. Really. So you want to get together?" I couldn't blame him if he told me to get lost.

"You don't seem to care about the project," he said.

"I do care. Honest. I want to get a good grade on this. Give me another chance, okay?"

The mention of grades seemed to do the trick. "I guess it wouldn't hurt," Ed said.

"Great. We'll work on it right after school. Let's grab a burger or something in town. Okay? My treat."

Ed nodded. Then he dashed ahead to catch up with Mr. Abruzzi. "I've been thinking about this all weekend. Do we get to pick out the charity, too?" he asked.

"Sure," Mr. Abruzzi said.

"I heard the Sharing Shepherd needs money," Ed told him.

The mention of that place reminded me of the man with the walrus mustache. Thoughts of him made my scalp tingle.

The sharp smell of fresh paint drifted down the hall, mixing oddly with the memories of the shelter. I saw Donny over on the left, with a scraper in one hand and a paint-brush in the other, removing some creative writing from a locker. I nodded and he nodded back. In a way, he had sort of a cool job, because he got to do all kinds of different things, and he was pretty much his own boss. As long as the building was clean and all the broken stuff got fixed, no-body bothered him.

Up ahead, Ed kept talking. "They do a lot of good work at the Sharing Shepherd. My church gives them money sometimes. My folks and I go there every Christmas to help serve dinner. Thanksgiving, too. And it's part of the com-munity. So we're helping our own neighbors. Right? And better yet, it all ties in with my idea. You see, the way we raise the funds is—"

"Slow down, Ed," Mr. Abruzzi said. "I appreciate your enthusiasm. But let's get to the room, first. Okay?"

"Okay." Ed looked back at me and smiled, which was pretty strange, since he'd just finished telling me how I'd let him down.

I didn't get it.

Then he winked.

I still didn't get it. And that worried me.

Then he mouthed the words, "Garage sale."

Oh crap. Now I got it. I'd promised that I'd support his idea. He was counting on my vote.

"After you, kids," Mr. Abruzzi said when we reached the meeting room.

I let Michelle go first. Then I walked in behind Ed, which seemed appropriate because, the way things were going, it looked like I was about to stab him in the back.

8

What's the Big Idea?

So," Mr. Abruzzi said after we'd taken seats around the large table that filled the room, "who wants to go first?"

I sighed and sat back, postponing the moment when I would turn into a rat. Ed's hand shot up. Michelle started to raise hers, then let it drop.

"Go ahead, Ed," Mr. Abruzzi said.

"You all know what a garage sale is," Ed began. Then he explained his idea, along with all the reasons the money should go to the Sharing Shepherd. Through the whole thing, he kept trying to catch my eye.

"Nice, Ed. Very well thought-out," Mr. Abruzzi said when Ed was done. "And definitely a worthy cause." He glanced around the table. "Any other suggestions?"

Ed grinned at me again, then shifted his gaze toward Michelle as she spoke.

"I had one idea that might be fun," she said. "But I'm not sure if it's any good."

"Go ahead," Mr. Abruzzi said. "No harm kicking it around."

"I was thinking of a fashion show. We could have categories. Your favorite shirt. The best outfits for watching a football game. The perfect clothes for the last day of school. Maybe even get some teachers on the runway. We could sell tickets, but we could also charge people to be in the show. A lot of kids would pay to see what it's like to be a model. I think that would be kinda fun."

"Interesting idea," Mr. Abruzzi said. "Very different, Michelle. And very creative."

"Maybe we could even do swimsuits," she added.

The silence that followed was ended by a loud gulp from Ed.

I had to admit, it was a pretty clever idea. I guess Ed was torn. He'd want us to pick his idea, but maybe he'd also want to vote for Michelle's idea. And I was about to shoot holes in both those plans. Too bad we couldn't combine it all. Unless . . .

"Yes!" I let out a gasp as I saw the solution. Everyone stared at me. Good grief—they probably thought I was gasping over the idea of a swimsuit show. Oh man, I could just see Mr. Abruzzi slipping a note in my permanent record—*gets overexcited at the thought of swimsuits.*

"Mercer, do you have anything for us?" Mr. Abruzzi asked.

"Yeah. I have something kinda cool." I flipped open the folder. Across the room, Ed's expression grew cold. Just give me a minute, I thought. I could make it work. I could make everyone happy. Not only that, but I'd also be making my own idea even better.

"I'm sure you're familiar with Wizards of the Warrior World," I said, finally launching into the talk I'd already given dozens of times in my mind.

At this point, they were supposed to nod. I guess they didn't know that. Their heads were shaking in the wrong direction.

"It's the game everyone plays," I explained.

No reaction.

"In study hall," I said, feeling like I'd suddenly found myself on another planet.

Mr. Abruzzi nodded now. He'd had his share of duty there. "It's a role-playing game," I told Michelle. Then I turned to Ed. "You saw it in my room. Remember?"

"Sorry," he said. "I forgot." He gave me a sarcastic smile.

I kept going. "Anyhow, it's real popular. Tons of kids play it. I was at a gaming session this weekend and the place was mobbed. It's not just fun to play. It's fun to watch. My idea is, we could have a game tournament. We charge a small admission for spectators, and charge a larger entry fee for players. We can get local businesses to donate prizes." I handed out the sheets in my folder. "Here's a layout of the whole thing in the gym, and some information from conventions all over the country, with attendance figures."

As they glanced at the papers, I launched into the part that I hoped would keep Ed from hating me. "We can combine this with Ed's idea to sell stuff. It fits together perfectly. We can bring in stores that sell gaming equipment. But we don't have to limit it to that. We can sell anything else the players might be interested in. And kids can bring gear that they want to swap or sell." I could see it now—the whole gym filled with fantasy items. There was a big bookstore across town. They could set up a booth with books by Tolkien and C. S. Lewis and all sorts of other cool writers. I knew I could find a place that would bring posters, too.

"Like an ancient market," Michelle said.

"Yeah! Exactly. A marketplace." I loved the idea. "We turn part of the gym into a bazaar. There's tons of room. We could make a market area with a couple streets. Like Morocco or something," I added, going for the geography connection. This was getting better and better. It wouldn't just be a tournament now. It would be a whole convention.

"I like that, Mercer," Mr. Abruzzi said. "A little Marrakesh, with haggling merchants. A taste of ancient Persia. A touch of Alexandria. A bit of Bombay. A mingling of times and places. There's just one question that worries me."

Uh-oh. "What?" I asked.

"Aren't we excluding a lot of people by having an event based on a game that not everyone plays?"

I was more glad than ever that I'd spent so much time preparing. "Not everyone plays chess," I said. "But they have chess tournaments. Right? Same with bridge, or any other game. Not everyone likes chocolate, for that matter. Some people are even allergic. But we sell chocolate. Besides, people who don't play are invited to come watch."

Mr. Abruzzi nodded. "Fair enough."

It was about to get even fairer. "And we can use Michelle's idea, too," I said.

"How?" she asked.

"We hold a contest for the best warrior costume. Or have a fantasy fashion show. It would be so cool."

Michelle nodded. "That sounds good. Except I still don't understand what this game's about."

I realized she didn't know anything about fantasy role-playing. "It's not complicated. You battle monsters, fight enemies, and cast spells."

"Spells?" Ed said, frowning at me. "What kind of spells?"

"Relax. It's all make-believe," I said. I turned toward Michelle. "It's a lot better to see the game than hear about it. We're playing next period. You have study hall, right?"

"Yeah."

"Great. I'll show you the whole thing." I turned toward Ed. "You want to take a look, too?"

"No, thanks," Ed said. "I already know what it's all about."

"Well, it seems we have a plan," Mr. Abruzzi said. "Shall we vote on it? Who would like to use Mercer's idea?"

"It's really everyone's idea," I said.

"Let's try it," Michelle said, raising her hand.

I raised my hand, too, and waited to see what Ed would do. I'd won, no matter how he voted. But I wanted him to feel good about the plan.

"Can I pick the charity?" Ed asked. "I'd really like to help the Sharing Shepherd."

Michelle nodded. So did I.

"Then it's settled?" Mr. Abruzzi asked.

"I guess." Ed sighed and raised his hand. That was a relief. I was afraid he was going to cause trouble.

"Great," Mr. Abruzzi said. "You need to get organized right away. This is a lot more involved than selling chocolate bars. But also a lot more interesting. I have to get the okay from the rest of the staff, but that's just a formality. And someone should tell the people who run the shelter about our plans."

"I can go there after school," Michelle said.

"You want to go along, Ed?" Mr. Abruzzi asked. "It was your idea to pick them."

"I'm not sure I can," Ed said. "I've got this thing after school. I guess it depends on how long it'll take. But maybe I shouldn't. With all the work I have, I really can't—"

"I'm free," I said. Shath'dra would never let the fair maiden go to the shelter unprotected. Neither could I. I wasn't exactly crazy about the idea of visiting the Sharing Shepherd, but I figured we could dash in, tell them about the fund-raiser, and then get right out. Besides, this was a chance to spend more time with Michelle.

"That okay with you?" Mr. Abruzzi asked her.

I halfway expected Michelle to turn me down, but she said, "Sure."

"Okay. Meeting adjourned," Mr. Abruzzi said.

Ed glared at me. I knew he wasn't happy about the vote, but that was no reason to get so angry. And then it hit me. Ed's after-school plans—they were with me. I'd just broken another promise. Before I could say anything else, he got up and stormed out of the room.

9

Welcome to
My Other World

On the way back, I tried to spot the locker where Donny had done his patchwork. I couldn't find it. That wasn't a surprise. Donny was a wizard with a paintbrush. He was great with just about any tool. I, on the other hand, seemed to be a wizard at screwing up. I hoped it wasn't too late to fix things. Too bad they didn't make repair paint for people.

When I got back to my desk, I tried to patch things up with Ed. "Why don't you come along? We can go to the shelter, then work on our paper."

"No, thanks," he said, not even bothering to turn around.

"Come on . . ."

Now he turned around and glared at me. "I don't have time. I have to do my column. As a matter of fact, I have to rewrite the whole thing. And I have a report to work on. *Somebody's* got to do it. Somebody with a sense of *responsi-*

bility. Not somebody who plays around with devil worship and witchcraft. I never should have voted for you. Especially not after you mentioned spells. Don't you know where that stuff comes from? That's black magic, Mercer. It's evil."

Man, we'd been through this already. "Ed, it's just a game. Lighten up. Come on. Go to the shelter with me and Michelle. All right? She wants you to come. Honest." I looked across the room toward Michelle to see if I could catch her eye.

"I've got too much real work to do," Ed said. "I don't have time to play games and run around acting like some girl's pet dog."

Ouch. That was a low blow. I wasn't anyone's pet dog. I was just being friendly. I let it go and gave my attention to Mr. Abruzzi. It would be easier to talk with Ed later, after we started working on the fund-raiser.

At the end of the period, Michelle and I walked down to room 157. When we got there, I told everyone the news.

"The man!" Drew said. "Way to go."

"Good job," Jenna said.

"Michelle needs to see what the game is like," I said.

"Want to play?" Kyle asked her. "That's the best way to learn."

"That's okay," Michelle said. "I'll just watch."

"Yeah," Jenna said. "She can't come in now. The game's already started." She put her elbows on the table and leaned forward, as if guarding her dice from attack.

"Sure she can," Kyle said. He handed Michelle his dice. "Here, pick your character and roll for your starting points."

Michelle smiled shyly at Jenna, as if waiting to make sure there were no more objections. Jenna wouldn't look back at her. Finally, Michelle created a character. She started out as a warrior with a touch of goddess blood and a talent for finding treasure. She named her character Blaze. Unfortunately, Blaze lasted about as long as a tiny spark.

When Jenna's first turn came, she said, "I hurl my spear at the female warrior." She threw her dice so hard, they bounced off the table and clattered to a stop on the floor, showing high numbers.

"Roll your dice," I told Michelle. "You need to see how well you defended against the attack."

Michelle rolled. Low numbers. Bad news.

"The spear flies true," Kyle said. "It's a deadly cast, passing straight through the heart." He broke out of his role of Game Lord long enough to say, "Sorry."

"I'm dead?" Michelle asked. "Just like that?"

"It happens," Drew told her.

"Nothing personal," Jenna said, giving Michelle an innocent grin. "I'd been dying to test my new spear, and there you were. No shield. No armor. All that soft and vulnerable flesh standing right in front of me. I couldn't resist."

"Look, this isn't fair," I said. "Michelle's just trying to see how the game's played. We shouldn't be throwing spears at her."

"Sorry," Jenna said. "Next time I'll use my crossbow."

I resisted the urge to chuck something at her. "That's not what I meant. You know you weren't being fair."

"Who made you Game Lord?" Jenna asked. She turned toward Kyle. "What do you say? I killed her fair and square, right?"

Before Kyle could answer, Michelle handed back the dice. I was afraid she was going to walk out. Instead, she settled in her chair and said, "I'll just watch for now. We're planning to have as many spectators as players, right? So let me see what it's like to be a spectator."

That made sense. We played, and Michelle watched. At one point I sneaked a peek in her direction and saw her smiling.

When the period ended, I asked her, "Well?"

"Yup," Michelle said. "Obviously, you won't have any trouble getting players to come. The trick is to let everyone else know it'll be fun. We have to make this into an *event*. Mention stuff like magic and monsters. We'll need lots of big, flashy posters."

"Great." I knew we were in good shape. Having Michelle on our team was like getting a sports star to promote a product.

"I'll meet you out front after school," she said.

I nodded.

"Got a date?" Jenna asked as Michelle left the room.

"We're going to the shelter."

"Wow—talk about a cheap date. Couldn't you at least buy her a hot dog from the cart in the park?"

"Give it a rest," I said. "We're going to check out a charity. That's all. What's your problem, anyhow?"

"I just don't want our game messed up. We don't need anyone new coming along. Especially not Miss Perfect. And we don't need anything changed. We all like things the way they are."

"Nothing's changing," I told her as I gathered up my gaming equipment. "No way Michelle would want to join us. Especially now, thanks to you and your spear. Look, we're going to have a convention and a tournament. That's something we all want, right?"

"I guess so," Jenna said. She glared toward the door. "But I still don't like her. I've got some real spells at home. How about I give her a face full of warts?"

"Forget that, Jenna. Help us with the convention. We need experienced players on the committee. There's a lot to figure out." I turned to the others. "And you guys, too. I'm going to need all the help I can get."

"I'm in," Kyle said.

"Me, too," Drew said.

Finally, Jenna said, "Oh shoot. Count me in. Just promise me things will go back to normal afterward."

"No problem," I said. "You've got my word." If I'd thought about it before I spoke, I would have realized I'd been racking up an extremely poor record at keeping my promises.

10

Meet Chuck

You know anything about this place?" Michelle asked when I met up with her after school.

"Not really." I still wasn't thrilled about going to the Sharing Shepherd. I thought about the woman who'd smiled at Tracy. She seemed nice. But I couldn't imagine talking with her. Or spending time with her. I wasn't proud of how I felt, but that didn't change things.

"Thanks for coming along," Michelle said.

I nodded, but kept my mouth shut to avoid saying something really stupid like, "Don't worry, I'll protect you," or, "I'm just happy to be with you." Instead, I turned my attention to avoiding tripping, stumbling, or walking into a tree. In Michelle's presence, even the simple task of breathing felt clumsy. It's hard to act normal when the only thing on your mind is trying to be natural.

Fortunately, I made it to the Sharing Shepherd without any unplanned acrobatics. I expected the place to be musty or smelly inside, like the used-book store, but when we stepped through the doorway, the most amazing aroma hit me. It smelled even better than Mom's bread.

I noticed a couple dozen people scattered among the tables. Some were reading newspapers or magazines. Some were talking. Others were just sitting there. Those who bothered to look up glanced at us with no sign of interest.

"Hi," I said, not talking to anyone in particular. My voice sounded out of place.

Nobody answered. I looked down and found myself staring at my fancy new sneakers.

"Now what?" Michelle asked.

I saw signs of movement in the back. "Let's try there." I crossed the room and went through large, open double doors. The aroma grew stronger.

A guy with frizzy brown hair gathered in a ponytail was stirring a huge pot that bubbled away on top of an old stove. He wore a food-splattered white apron and a blue baseball cap with a picture of Mickey Mouse above the brim.

"Excuse me," I said, walking toward him.

The guy grinned at us and let go of the large wooden spoon. It remained straight up in the thick mixture. "Hiya," he said. He wiped his hand on the apron, glanced at it, wiped it again, and then thrust it out. "I'm Pastor Chuck. Welcome."

"Hi," I said as I shook his hand. From the strength of his grip, I figured he spent a lot of time stirring big pots of food.

Michelle took her turn shaking his hand. "We're from the middle school."

"That's a relief," Pastor Chuck said. "I thought you were from the Internal Revenue Service." He grinned again, and I realized he was joking.

"You kids hungry?" he asked.

"No, thanks." I shook my head.

"It's my specialty," he said. "My own recipe. I call it Chuck steak. Since that's my name and all. Here. You have to try it." He grabbed a couple spoons from a drawer and gave us each a bite.

"Great," I said. It tasted even better than it smelled.

"Delicious," Michelle said.

"Thank you. But if you're not hungry and you're not from the federal government, what brings you here?" he asked.

"The eighth grade at the middle school holds a fundraiser each year," Michelle said.

"We're having a gaming convention," I added.

"We donate whatever we make to a good cause," Michelle said. "Someone on our committee suggested the Sharing Shepherd. We wanted to make sure it was okay with the people in charge."

Pastor Chuck looked slowly from Michelle to me. "So what you're saying is that you want my permission to give me money?"

Michelle and I nodded.

"I'll have to think about that," he said. "Can I get back to you, say maybe by Friday?"

"Sure," I said. "Friday would be . . ." I stopped when I realized he was kidding again.

"Money would be wonderful," Pastor Chuck told us. "I thank you from the bottom of my heart. We'll take any help we can get. Money. Groceries. Labor. You know, if someone volunteered to do a bit of washing," he said, nodding toward a stack of dishes, pots, and pans overflowing a sink to our right, "I'd consider myself blessed."

Oh man. I didn't even wash dishes at home. But Pastor Chuck was the kind of guy who was hard to let down. I looked at Michelle and she shrugged. "I've got four brothers," she said. "I'm used to messes."

"What the heck," I said. Then I gritted my teeth and glanced at Pastor Chuck. "Sorry."

"No sweat. You wash those pots, you can say *heck* as much as you want. I'll even throw in a couple *darn*s and a *drat*. But nothing stronger. Deal?"

"Deal."

Michelle and I got to work.

"I'll be back in a minute. I have some food to deliver,"

Pastor Chuck said, picking up a large shopping bag. He pointed at the simmering stew. "If that explodes, the mops are in the closet." He jogged out of the kitchen.

"I think he's kidding," I said.

"Hope so," Michelle said.

So there I was, up to my elbows in suds, grease, and food particles, standing next to the most beautiful girl in the school and trying to think of something interesting to talk about. I was saved from silence when she asked me to tell her more about the game and how the magic worked.

"It takes power to cast spells," I said. "But also experience and dexterity. Magic is an art. The same spell in different hands can have different effects." I glanced at her to make sure her eyes weren't glazing over. The last thing I wanted was to bore her. But she seemed interested. So I kept on talking, telling her tales of wizards and spells, losing myself in the sound of my own words and the rhythm of scrubbing the pots.

"I guess you like being a wizard," she said as we finished rinsing the last couple dishes.

"Absolutely. It's great being a wizard." As I spoke, I sensed someone behind me. I looked over my shoulder, then spun around.

The man with the walrus mustache and beat-up black cowboy hat was staring at me. I had no idea how long he'd been listening. He stepped closer and waved something in my face. I tried to move back, but the sink was right behind me. The hard, wet edge pressed into the base of my spine.

Next to me, Michelle let out a gasp.

The guy waved his hand again. No mistake. He was holding a knife.

11

No More Mr. Knife Guy

Shath'dra would have melted the knife with a quicksilver spell. I didn't have that option. I didn't have a shield or armor, either. All I had was a plastic scrubbee thing and a nearly empty bottle of dish detergent. Maybe someone more talented could make a weapon out of that, but not me. *Stand back or I'll scour you?*

"Make us!" the man shouted.

"Get away," I said.

"Calm down," Michelle told him.

Ignoring both requests, he drew his arm back and raised the knife, clutching the handle so hard, I could see the veins in his wrist bulge out. It was a butter knife, not a sharp kitchen knife, but that didn't make me feel any better.

He looked away from me and stared at the knife. Then he screamed again. It didn't sound like words this time. It was more like a wail, or a weird song. Adding to the weirdness, he patted himself on the head with his other hand, flattening the top of his cowboy hat.

Michelle clutched my arm. The man thrust his hand out, holding it open with the knife lying across his palm. His fingers jabbed against my chest. Right then, Pastor Chuck came running back into the kitchen.

"Hurko," he said in a calm voice. "What's the problem?"

The man—I guess his name was Hurko—tried to hide the knife, but Pastor Chuck snatched it from him. "Oh, I see what's wrong." He waggled the knife, showing us a sharp bend in the middle of the blade. I hadn't noticed that before. But a crooked utensil sure wasn't something worth getting bent out of shape over.

"It's okay," Pastor Chuck said. "We've got plenty of knives. There's no reason to be upset. Just get yourself another one." He gave Hurko a pat on the back.

The man started to say something, but Pastor Chuck interrupted him. "We'll talk later, after our new friends leave. Go back to your table. The food will be ready soon."

Hurko scurried out.

"Sorry," Pastor Chuck said. "I hope he didn't scare you."

"That's okay," I said, trying to stop all my nerves from buzzing like a thousand electric razors on caffeine. I glanced over at Michelle. "You all right?"

She nodded.

"He's not dangerous," Pastor Chuck said. "He's just a little different from us. But that's why he's here. If he fit in, he wouldn't need help. Though I have to admit, the four of them are a bit more different than our usual guests."

"Four?" I asked.

Pastor Chuck nodded. "Hurko and his friends showed up about six months ago. They stick pretty close together. If I had to guess, based on their accents, I'd say they're from somewhere in eastern Europe. Maybe Lithuania or Hungary. But I might be wrong about that. I've tried to get them jobs, but they have a rough time coping." He sighed, then said, "I hope this won't make you change your mind about that donation."

I glanced over at Michelle. She shook her head. "You're doing good work," she said. "This is the right place for the money."

"Thanks," Pastor Chuck said.

"Can we go that way?" I asked, pointing to a door at the rear of the kitchen. I didn't want to run into Hurko again, especially not if he was with his three friends.

"Sure can. You'll have to climb the fence to get to the street, but it's an easy one. You did a great job with the pots. Come back anytime."

We headed out. A tall wooden fence blocked the end of the alley. It had a couple missing slats, but none of the gaps was wide enough to fit through. There was an old crate—the kind that oranges come in—at the bottom of the fence. Michelle put one foot on the crate, hopped up, and vaulted over the fence.

My turn. In my mind, I saw myself sailing across with a graceful flip and half twist. I backed up a couple steps, dashed forward, and leaped onto the box—which broke under my weight as I grabbed the top of the fence, leaving me hanging and swaying like overalls on a clothesline.

"You okay?" Michelle called from the other side. I could see her all too clearly through one of the gaps. That meant she could see me, too.

"Just fine," I said, trying not to grunt from the effort of scrambling over the fence. I got one leg up, then managed to roll my body to the other side without permanently damaging anything important.

"Wow," Michelle said when I'd joined her, "that was scary." She didn't say a word about my lack of climbing skills. Jenna, Kyle, or anyone else I knew would have made jokes for hours.

"Yeah," I admitted. "That guy was spooky." I thought about those blazing eyes, and wondered if he saw a different world than I did.

"I'm glad we're giving them the money," Michelle said.

"You are?" I was just glad to get away from there.

"Sure. I think it's the people we don't want to be around who need our help the most."

"That doesn't make it any easier," I said.

"I guess not. But it makes it more important."

As she spoke, it struck me that I was doing something I'd never imagined I'd do. I was walking through town with the prettiest girl in school, having a serious discussion about important subjects. We'd just faced down danger together—well, we'd faced down bent silverware, but still it was something.

12

Ed Fled

The next day, in geography, Ed dropped a stack of paper on my desk. "Here's our English project," he said. "It's all done. Congratulations, you're going to get a great grade."

I stared down at the title: "The Pilgrim Meets Parsifal." Four words that meant absolutely nothing to me. "You could have waited. I told you we'd work together."

"You can do the cover," he said. "If you can find the time."

That was Ed's first surprise for me that day. The second came at the end of class when Mr. Abruzzi called us up to his desk.

"I'd like to schedule a meeting for lunchtime," he said.

"Lunchtime is good," I said, relieved that I wouldn't miss my game.

"Yeah, that's fine," Michelle said.

"What about you, Ed?" Mr. Abruzzi asked.

"I have to quit the committee," Ed said. "I have a conflict."

"Are you sure, Ed?" Mr. Abruzzi asked. "You've made a big contribution. There's plenty more you can do. We'd miss you if you dropped out."

"I have a conflict," Ed said again. "Sorry. There's nothing I can do about it." He gave me an odd look, then left the room.

I should have been thrilled. It was just me and Michelle now. But I felt rotten. I wondered how much of Ed's decision was my fault. Was I his conflict?

"Too bad," Michelle said. "He really could have helped."

"You two will just have to fill in the gap," Mr. Abruzzi said. "I suggest you find as many volunteers as you can and divide the work. For starters, why not split the whole thing down the middle? Mercer, you take care of everything to do with the game, and Michelle, you handle everything to do with spectators, merchants, and so on. How's that sound?"

"Fine," I said.

"Sounds good," Michelle said.

"I'll give you a couple days to get organized." He glanced at the calendar on his desk. "Let's say we meet on Thursday during lunch. Okay?"

We agreed to that, then headed out. When I reached the study hall, I asked the others if they'd mind spending some time working on ideas for the convention. They were happy to help. By the end of the period, I felt we had everything under control.

That night, I read Ed's paper. I couldn't bring myself to think of it as *our* paper, even if my name was there with his under the title. It was good. Better than I could have done on my own. One of the characters was this knight named Parsifal, who was in a story about King Arthur and the search for the Holy Grail. Ed had put him together with this guy named Christian from a book called *The Pilgrim's Progress*. He'd set them in this story where Christian was an antiques dealer on a television show, and Parsifal was bringing him the Grail to get an appraisal.

I searched without luck for anything I could improve. Ed really knew how to write. I hated taking half the credit when he'd done all the work. I wondered whether he thought about me the same way I thought about Dooley Cronk and all the other kids whose work I'd done.

Well, there was one small thing I could do. The report still needed a cover. I spent over two hours trying to make it as spectacular as possible. It wasn't good enough to wash away my guilt, but I had to admit it looked pretty great. I printed out the cover, finished the rest of my homework, and got ready for bed. Pushing aside thoughts of the English project, I let my mind wander through scenes of the convention.

This is going to be so cool, I thought as I fell asleep.

In the morning, on the way to my homeroom, I grabbed a copy of our school paper, *The Wilde Times*, from one of the bins by the front door. I didn't look at it until I reached my desk, but I should have guessed from the way people stared at me in the hall that something was going on.

When I opened the paper, I found out that Ed had a third surprise for me. And this one was a whopper.

13

A Heck of a Column

It was on page three, lurking between an article about the athlete of the week and a movie review. Ed's column. "(h)E(a)D Lines," by Ed Bingham. The headline read: "Demons Stalk the Halls." Below that was another sentence: *Could a seemingly innocent game be a road to destruction?*

"Oh crap," I muttered as I started reading. Ed had written his column about Wizards of the Warrior World. According to him, the game stole time from studies and distracted students from getting their assignments done. But all of that was just a warm-up for his real objections. He was disturbed by the "fascination with demons and demonic trappings." The players were, according to him, "playing dice with their souls." Man. Nice shot, Ed. I guess he'd decided to get me back for anything he thought I'd done to him. He really went all-out in the last paragraph:

Despite repeated assurances from players that all of this is "just a game," the truth is much darker. Every aspect of the game is derived from Satanic sources. The magic system is thinly disguised sorcery. This game world is filled with demons and spirits. This system accepts dark forces and at the same time denies the existence of one true God. Worse, each player acts in the most immoral fashion imaginable. Thievery, deceit, murder, and other sinister practices are encouraged and rewarded. There is no rule of *Love your neighbor* in this world. This is not "just a game." It is a training ground for damnation.

At the bottom of the column, set off from everything else, he'd written, "This game must be stopped. It's time to get the devil out of here."

Sheesh. I put the paper down and checked around the room. It was obvious most of the kids were talking about the column. "You see this?" I asked Kyle.

He nodded. "No big deal. Who pays attention to the Head?"

"You think it's nothing?"

"Sure. Everyone'll get a laugh over it, but that's all. And they won't be laughing at us—they'll be laughing at him. Demonic trappings? Sinister practices? Give me a break."

It turned out Kyle was right. From what I could tell, everything was blowing over pretty quickly. On the way to my first-period class, I got kidded a couple times by people who knew I was a game player. Barty Mills called me "Demon Boy," and Runt Ronkowski backed away from me in mock terror, shouting, "Keep your devil dice to yourself!"

Between first and second period, I got kidded once. By third period, nobody was mentioning the game. As I walked into geography class, I almost felt sorry for Ed. He'd taken his best shot, and it had fallen to the ground about two feet from the mouth of the cannon.

I wasn't sure what I'd say to him. Or if I'd say anything at all. The article was personal. He was trying to hurt me. I figured the best strategy was to act like it didn't bother me at all.

"Great report," I said, dropping the English project on his desk. "You sure I can't add anything?"

"It's done," he said, glancing down at the cover. "Forget about it." He shifted his eyes toward my copy of *The Wilde Times*, then looked back at me.

"Interesting column," I said.

"If that's your only response, maybe you'd better read it more closely," Ed said.

"I don't really have any response," I told him. "Neither does anyone else around here."

"In that case, I guess I need to find a more receptive audience," he said. He turned back around in his seat. Class started and I let the whole thing drop.

I got real busy after that. Michelle and I picked a date

for the convention, deciding on a Saturday four weeks away, which we figured would give us lots of time. We had plenty of student volunteers. A couple teachers pitched in, too. Ms. MacIntosh let me spend all my art time making models and decorations. She even got permission to leave the back door unlocked for me so I could go in after dinner. That was okay, since Donny was usually around pretty late.

Soon, everyone was building papier-mâché statues. We raided the recycling bin for newspapers, which was kind of weird, since it was Ed who'd started the recycling program. I almost felt like I was stealing from him.

Thursday, we met with Mr. Abruzzi, and he approved our plans. We also decided it would be a good idea for the student committee to meet each Friday.

I stayed really late all of the next week. The art room was cool. It's actually a double room, with the middle wall removed. There are tables for drawing, easels for painting, a pottery wheel, a kiln, silk screen frames, and just about everything anyone would need to do all sorts of projects.

Sometimes, I'd snack on an apple while I worked. Ms. MacIntosh kept a huge bowl of them on her desk. Kyle had brought her an apple at the start of the year as kind of a joke, since McIntosh is a type of apple and since kids used to give apples to their teachers. The joke caught on and other kids started doing it. So she got this bowl, and anyone who wanted an apple could help himself.

I felt sort of bad because we'd made such a mess with all

the flour and water we'd used for the papier-mâché. Donny walked through one night as I was getting ready to leave. I'd cleaned up as much as I could, but the floor and table still didn't look great.

"Sorry," I said. "Want me to stay?"

"Nah, go on home, kid. I've got it covered." He twirled his mop and smiled.

"You sure?" I dusted off my hands, sending a small cloud of flour drifting through the air. For a moment, it dimmed the evening sunlight coming through the window.

Donny looked at the statues that were taking over the room. "I'm sure. You've been working plenty hard."

"Thanks." I headed out.

On Friday, the committee members met at lunch. "The booth space has all been sold," Michelle said, looking down at her list. "I was surprised how much fantasy stuff I found. There'll also be a swap area for kids who want to sell or trade things."

"Decorations are coming along," I said. I pointed around the cafeteria, where we'd placed a couple posters and three of the statues. That was Michelle's idea. We'd put statues all over the school, to help build excitement for the tournament.

"The comic store donated door prizes," Drew said.

"Good," Michelle said. "What about publicity?"

Kyle had volunteered to handle that because his parents owned a print shop. "I've got the flyers designed," he told the group. "I'll finish them this weekend. Jenna and I are going to ask the local radio stations to give us a mention."

"How about the *Cryer*?" Michelle asked, mentioning our daily newspaper. "Can you get them to run something?"

Kyle shook his head. "I'll see what I can do. But it's really tough. There are too many towns around here, and everyone has things going on. It would be a miracle to get any kind of mention from them."

"Well," Michelle said, "try your best."

"Sure. Just don't get your hopes up," Kyle said.

But Monday, when the protesters appeared, I discovered we'd already gotten more publicity, and more attention, than we'd ever asked for.

14

Demon-Stration

I heard it fifth period during my law and government class. For a minute or two, the sound just passed through my ears, trickled around my brain, and moved on. Then, slowly, it started tapping against the wall of my consciousness. A chant.

Ya da DADA yada DAH!
Ya da DADA yada DAH!

I listened more carefully and found words inside the chant.

Get the DADA yada DAH!

Quietly, I slid my chair toward the window and leaned close to the glass for a better look. Fifteen or twenty people were marching in a messy oval on the sidewalk, waving hand-painted signs tacked to posts. They were the source of the noise.

Get the devil outta here!

Call me dense—but for a wonderfully peaceful three or four seconds, I didn't make the connection between them and me. It was fun looking down from the window. The way the glass muffled the sound, I felt like I was watching a TV news broadcast with the volume turned low.

Some of the people were waving a page from a newspaper. I recognized the *Cryer* as it fluttered like trapped doves clutched in a half dozen fists.

Around the fifth second or so, I realized that the messages on the signs seemed familiar. So did the chant. Where had I heard it before?

Somewhere before the tenth second slipped past, my brain finally handed me an explanation. "Oh crap!" I shouted at the same unfortunate moment Mr. Soloski paused for breath.

My voice echoed in the room. Like it or not, I had everyone's attention—especially my teacher's.

"Mercer, what's so fascinating out the window?" he asked.

Under normal circumstances, the only safe response to that question was, "Nothing. Sorry." And the only safe action was to turn my attention back to the lesson. But this was pretty far from normal circumstances. I pointed outside and waited for Mr. Soloski to walk over.

"Good lord," he muttered when he reached the window. "They're picketing the school."

Naturally, that brought the whole class rushing to join us. I watched Principal Calvert step out of the building and speak with one of the protesters. They exchanged words for a minute, then the principal threw his hands in the air and walked back inside.

"I think we just witnessed a First Amendment discussion," Mr. Soloski said. He let us hover by the windows while he explained the concept of freedom of expression.

Now I understood what Ed had meant when he'd talked about finding a more receptive audience. He must have sent his column to the paper. And, amazingly, they'd printed it. Which gave those wackos outside a chance to read it. I walked over to Ed and asked, "Friends of yours?"

He shook his head. "Never seen them before."

"Well, they've seen you before. Looks like they're big fans of your column. They've got half the crap you wrote painted on those signs they're carrying."

The insult didn't seem to bother him. Instead, Ed's lips twitched toward a smile. "I wasn't sure I was good enough to get my writing in the *Cryer*. Not yet. This is *great*."

"Great? Are you kidding? You screwed stuff up for the whole school. You might think you're so smart and superior, but you're ruining things for everyone." I was tired of pretending Ed's attack didn't bother me. And tired of being nice.

I walked back to Mr. Soloski and asked him, "Can they do that?"

"The sidewalk is public property," he said. "They have the right to gather there, as long as they don't disrupt the school. Hey, why talk when we can interact? This is a perfect opportunity to view our system of social protest at close range. Come on—let's go meet the protesters."

Mr. Soloski herded us down the hall. Ed was so eager to get there, he dashed ahead. I took my time. When I finally reached the front door, the chant washed over me.

Outside, I hung toward the back of our group, almost certain that the mob would take one look at me and know I was the focus of their protests. I felt I had *Demon Boy* painted on my forehead in huge red letters.

A large, sweaty man in a brown suit, white shirt, and skinny black necktie raced toward us, waving a Bible in one hand. His hair was greased up and combed back in a bad Elvis impersonation. "Sir! It is imperative that you listen to me," he said to Mr. Soloski. "There are children at risk. We know what is occurring in your hallways, and we've come to stop it. We've come to save you from this iniquity. To cast out demons and heal sick minds. We come fulfilling the great commission."

Mr. Soloski shrugged. "We've come to watch."

I noticed a large white van parked across the street, along with a bunch of other cars and vans. *Church of the Light and Truth* was painted on the side of the large van. Underneath, in smaller letters, it said, *Reverend Willum Oakford*.

"If anyone corrupts a child such as these," the reverend shouted, "it would be better if a millstone were hung around his neck and he were dropped into the sea."

"Huh?" Kyle said from his spot next to me. "Millstone? Wasn't that a president's middle name or something? What's this guy talking about?"

"I think he wants to drown game players," I said, cringing at the image of sinking to the bottom of the sea.

"You do realize this is a public school?" Mr. Soloski said, sounding amazingly calm. "Religious arguments aren't relevant."

"And what is that demonic game," the reverend shouted, "but a twisted and perverse religion? You banish the Word. You banish prayer. You banish the true faith. But nonetheless, you have religion in your halls. You have praise and worship. But it is the praise of demons and the worship of darkness. It is the religion of Satan. Don't cast dice!" he shouted. "Cast out demons!"

Man, that was another line from Ed's column. The whole crowd pointed at us as they picked up the chant. "Don't cast dice!"

Every single finger seemed aimed directly at me.

I wanted to tell them it was just a game. But there was no way I was opening my mouth. I could almost imagine them tying me to a stake—or a highly flammable papier-mâché statue—and setting a fire at my feet.

"Maybe we'll wander back inside," Mr. Soloski said, much to my relief.

As we headed toward the door, I looked over at Ed, hoping that he'd realize how crazy all of this was now that he'd gotten a close-up view. But he seemed thrilled by the power his words had with his new fan club.

Five minutes later, the loudspeaker crackled. "Attention," the principal said, "there will be a special meeting after school for anyone involved in the upcoming fund-raiser."

"We're screwed," I said, sinking down in my chair. I could see the convention vanishing like a drop of water touched by the tip of a paper towel.

15

Flipped Out

Right after school, all the kids on the committee crowded into the office, along with Mr. Abruzzi.

"We have a situation on our hands," Principal Calvert said. He sighed and shook his head. "If this many people are disturbed by the plans, perhaps it would be best to cancel the fund-raiser."

"You can't," I said. Loudly.

Principal Calvert stared at me. Compared to the picketing reverend and his millstones, the principal wasn't all that scary. So I kept talking. "We've done a ton of work. People have already reserved booths. We can't tell them not to come. Besides, those protesters probably don't even have kids in this school." I desperately tried to think of any argument that would help our side.

"We have rights," Jenna said.

Principal Calvert didn't even glance at her.

"If we bow to religious pressure, we could be opening ourselves up to a lawsuit," Mr. Abruzzi said.

Good one. There was nothing better than having a teacher come to the rescue.

"You think so?" Principal Calvert asked.

Mr. Abruzzi nodded. "We can't let a loud minority dictate our actions."

"Or violate our rights," Jenna said.

"But what if other parents have objections?" Principal Calvert said. "We have to keep community standards in mind." He paused to thumb through an appointment calendar, then said, "The school board meets Wednesday evening. This is really a matter for them to deal with."

Well, that stunk. He'd decided to let someone else make the decision. But at least he hadn't killed the convention before giving us a chance to tell our side.

"Think we're in trouble?" I asked Mr. Abruzzi as we left the office.

He shrugged. "It's hard to say. That mob out there could have a whole different cause to scream about by Wednesday."

"We could tell them Darwin's been spotted across the river," Jenna suggested.

Mr. Abruzzi smiled at her. "We'll save that strategy for

an emergency. Bear one thing in mind—it may turn out that most parents around here don't like the idea of this game. If that's what we find, we have to respect their feelings."

Man, I hoped that wasn't the case. We'd been working too hard to see everything go up in a puff of righteous smoke.

The picketers were still outside when I left. So were some photographers, and a van from the local TV news station. Great. Their side was getting all the attention. What was wrong with these people? Did I go to their church and tell them which songs they could sing? What gave them the right to tell me which games I could play?

I wanted to avoid the picketers, so I started to cut across the lawn. But I spotted Jenna arguing with a man who was holding a sign that read, "Just Say 'No' to Satan!" She was wearing a shirt covered with astrological symbols, and a pendant with the figure of an Egyptian goddess. Great. That's all we needed. Let them think the whole school was overrun with Wiccans, Druids, reincarnated pharaohs, and Earth Mothers. Then they'd never go away.

I could hear her chattering as I moved closer. "Look, you think you have all the answers?" she said. "Well, then, answer me this. If God can do anything, can he make a stone so big, he can't move it? Huh? Can he? Got an answer? I mean, either he can do everything or he can't. But if he can make the stone, then he can't move it. But if he can move it, then he can't make it. See? Come on, answer me. I'm waiting."

Before the man could speak, she said, "And what about Cain? He goes off and gets married. Right? Who does he marry? Explain that one to me. We've got Adam and Eve. Next thing you know, Cain's off somewhere getting hitched. Where did the bride come from? A catalog? Did he mail order her from brides-dot-com? Or did he make her out of twigs and mud?"

The man finally opened his mouth, but Jenna was on a roll. "And another thing. Do you know how much violence has been done in the name of organized religion? Ever heard of the Crusades? Or the Inquisition? Let's not even talk about the Children's Crusade. I'm a pacifist. Peace is my religion. Do you have any idea how many people have been killed or hurt just because—"

I hurried over and grabbed her arm, hoping to pull her away. As usual, my body was a half second ahead of my brain, which had forgotten about her karate lessons. I flew briefly through the air, and ended on the ground with my elbow twisted the wrong way and Jenna's foot pressing against my throat.

"Oh, hi, Mercer." She released my arm, removed her heel from my windpipe, and stepped back. "You startled me. Thought I was being mugged."

"That's okay." As I got up, I noticed that the picketer

was staring at us like we were an alien life-form. Risking further injury or unplanned air travel, I dragged Jenna away, saying, "I need to talk with you."

"What's up?" she asked.

I couldn't tell her I was trying to keep her from making us a permanent target of every church in town, so I said, "I'm just checking up on your progress. Anything new for the tournament?"

"You bet." Jenna smiled, reached into her jacket pocket, and pulled out something that looked like a golf ball without the dimples. "I made this in the science lab today. Figured we could add some dazzle to the tournament."

"What is it?"

"Watch." She threw the ball onto the sidewalk by my feet.

"Whoa!" I jumped back as it exploded with a flash and a bang, releasing a large cloud of white smoke.

"Cool?" Jenna asked.

"Cool," I admitted.

"Got the formula from an old magic book. Stage magic. Not the real kind. They had all the chemicals I needed in the science lab—magnesium, potassium nitrate, and the rest. But don't tell our friends over there it's not witchcraft. I'd hate to let them down when they already think so badly of me. Here," Jenna said, pulling another of the balls from her pocket. "Take one. See if you can think up some ways we can use them."

"Thanks." I put the ball in my own jacket pocket.

"Gotta run," Jenna said. "See you tomorrow."

"See you."

I headed home. The smell of fresh-baked bread greeted me when I walked inside. "How was school?" Mom asked as I tore off a hunk of sourdough rye.

"The usual," I said through a mouthful of crust.

"Nothing out of the ordinary?" she asked, looking up at me from the table, where she was reading the newspaper.

The newspaper. Oh no. Even worse, I realized the little TV on the counter was tuned to the local news channel. "Well, I've got a ton of homework," I said as I headed for the stairs.

"Mercer," Mom called before I'd taken two steps.

I turned back and looked at her. "Can we talk later?" I asked.

She nodded. "Sure. But I need to know what's going on."

At least she didn't seem upset. I escaped to my room and switched on the computer. The first rule of combat is, Know your enemy. I wanted to see what I could find about protests against role-playing games. I also wanted to see if there were any laws that could help. I couldn't believe a group of strangers had the power to stop our fund-raiser.

I was surprised by how much information was out there. Church groups had been attacking game players since way back in the 1970s when Dungeons & Dragons was first getting popular. As for the law, that was so messed up, I couldn't figure anything out. There were state laws, local laws, and federal laws, along with constitutional rights and a mess of other stuff. No wonder there were so many lawyers.

After about an hour, my head started to feel overloaded. I logged off, sat back in my chair, and closed my eyes. Just then, the doorbell rang. A moment later, Mom called from below. "Mercer, are you up there?"

"I'm in my room," I called back.

"There's someone here to see you," she said.

"Who?" I asked as I walked toward the stairs. I figured it was Kyle or Drew. Or maybe Ed had stopped by to put me on a torture rack and stretch out a confession.

"A reporter from the *Cryer*," Mom said. "It seems that someone wants to hear about your perfectly ordinary day."

16

Press Start

I guess I expected some old guy with an unlit cigar clamped in the corner of his mouth and a crumpled hat jammed on his head. But the reporter was a woman who looked like she'd only been out of college a couple years.

"Hello, Mercer," she said. "I'm Sherry Windsor, with the *Daily Cryer*. I'm writing about the protests over at Oscar Wilde Middle School. Your name keeps popping up. You mind if I ask you some questions?" She'd already pulled out a notepad and pen.

"I guess not." I'd never talked to a reporter before.

"You play a game called"—she glanced down at her pad—"Wizards of the Warrior World. Is that right?"

"A lot of us play it," I said.

"Tell me about it."

So I described the game and explained about the convention. I made sure to point out we were raising money for a good cause. She asked some more questions about the game and about why I liked to play. We talked—well, mostly I talked—for over an hour. It was weird. I'd never had an adult really listen to me before. Not like this. She gave me all her attention. It made me nervous to realize someone was treating my words so seriously.

Mom hovered behind us the whole time, watching but not interrupting, except once to offer the reporter some bread.

Finally, when the interview was over, Ms. Windsor pulled out a cell phone and said, "Thank you for your time, Mercer. I'll arrange for one of our photographers to stop by if that's okay with you." She glanced at Mom, who nodded.

As Ms. Windsor walked to the door, I asked her, "So, what do you think?"

"I won't really know until I'm finished. I've got a couple more interviews to do. Then I'll have to read over all my notes. I guess we'll both find out what I think when tomorrow's paper hits the stands." She smiled and left.

Mom cleared her throat.

"I'm not doing anything wrong," I told her.

"I know. But be careful. People get crazy about stuff like this."

"You've got that right." I sat with her in the kitchen and described my day, so she could see just how crazy it had been. She told me she'd done a little protesting herself, about ten years ago, after some people started burning books they didn't like. Mom was no fan of fanatics.

A few minutes later, the photographer showed up. We went to my room, where he had me stand and sit in all kinds of poses.

I got to repeat everything for Dad during dinner. He didn't seem too worried, either. It was nice to have parents who trusted me.

Tomorrow should be interesting, I thought when I went to bed. Normally, I sleep until Mom gets me up for breakfast. But this morning, I was wide-awake an instant after the paper thumped against the porch. I ran out and brought the *Cryer* into the kitchen.

I found myself on page three of the second section. Wow. It was weird seeing my picture in the paper. But the photographer had picked a pretty cool shot. I was standing with my arms folded, leaning against my bookcase. You could make out some of the titles, like *Advanced Magic* and *A Guide to High Level Earth and Fire Spells*. The headline said, "Young Wizard Wants to Use Magic to Feed the Hungry." The caption under the picture mentioned that I was standing next to part of my extensive collection of wizard's equipment.

Another article on the same page described the protest, including more hellfire and millstones from Reverend Oakford. Ms. Windsor had also gone to the Sharing Shepherd. Pastor Chuck told her he had no idea what was going on and wasn't planning to comment about anything until he knew all the facts.

Oh man. My stomach churned as I read that part. If Reverend Oakford's church hated our game, maybe Pastor Chuck felt the same way. I couldn't remember how much I'd told him about the fund-raiser. I wasn't even sure whether I'd mentioned any details about the game. Either way, he must think I was some kind of troublemaker. One day, I'm telling him we're going to give him money, then the next thing he knows, a reporter shows up. I had to talk to him. Right now. We needed him on our side.

It was still pretty early, but I grabbed my school stuff and dashed out the door. I found Pastor Chuck in the kitchen of the Sharing Shepherd, along with a towering pile of dishes. I guess he'd already served breakfast.

"Hey, great timing, my friend," he said when he spotted me.

"I can't stay," I told him. "I have school. But I need to explain what's happening."

"I saw the official version," he said, pointing to a copy of the *Cryer* on the counter next to the sink. "Don't worry. I only believe half of what I read in the paper."

"There's a group who doesn't want us to have the convention," I said. "They think this is some kind of demon thing."

"What do you think?" he asked.

"It's just a game," I told him. "What about you? What do you think?"

"Ever read Romans?" he asked.

I shook my head. I'd studied about the Romans in school, but I didn't think that's what he was talking about.

"Hang on." He opened a closet and knelt by a stack of books on the bottom shelf. "Corinthians . . . Hebrews . . . *Harry Potter*. How'd that get in here? Ah, here we go." He pulled out a thin paperback. "Romans, with commentary. Check it out."

"Thanks." I slipped the book into my backpack. "So you aren't against the tournament?"

"I'm against hunger," he said. "I'm against people being tossed out like they're disposable. I'm against sin and evil, but it's not my place to judge what's in your heart. I have a hard enough time figuring out what's in my own heart. So, what time does school start?"

"Eight-thirty," I said, caught off guard by his sudden change of topic. Man, talking to him was like watching TV while someone else flipped through the channels.

"Well, that's a break. You've got plenty of time," he said, glancing at the clock and then at the sink. "And I've got plenty of dishes."

I sighed, rolled up my sleeves, and tackled the stack. It was a learning experience. I learned that after oatmeal sits for a certain period of time, it becomes virtually identical to concrete. A little while later, after he'd peeled a bunch of carrots and potatoes, Pastor Chuck ran off, saying something about picking up a donation of clothing. When I finished the dishes, I headed out the back door to the alley.

As I reached the fence, I heard footsteps behind me. Even before I spun around, I knew who I'd find. It was him again—Hurko. But he wasn't alone. This time, he'd brought his friends.

17

De-fence

Hurko rushed toward me. His friends—a man and two women—followed behind him. I glanced over my shoulder at the crate I'd smashed the other day. It was useless to me now. If I tried to pull myself over the fence, the four of them could grab my legs and drag me to the ground. Once they had me on my back, it would all be over except for the stomping.

"Get away," I shouted, holding out my hand.

Hurko froze for a second, then yelled, "Make us!"

The three of them crowded around him, as if they'd gathered for the world's weirdest family photograph. The other guy was young, but big. He looked strong enough to toss me right over the fence. His hair was shaggy, like he'd cut it himself with a pocketknife. He was wearing a maroon sports jacket, green plaid flannel shirt, jeans, and a Nike headband.

One of the women was small and thin, with hair just starting to turn gray. Her flowered skirt clashed weirdly with a red sweatshirt and a pair of hiking boots. The other woman, dressed in overalls, was young with very long hair and a face I'd probably think was pretty if she wasn't part of a crowd that was about to attack me. Beneath the overalls, she had on a blue dress shirt with a smile button pinned to the collar. Whatever fashion statement the group was trying to make, it wasn't working.

Hurko muttered something to the older woman. She bent and grabbed a rock from the ground. Then she shouted in that wailing way, like Hurko had done the other day in the kitchen, and slapped herself on the cheek with her free hand.

"Hey!" I ducked as she threw the rock at me. It shot past my head and hit the fence with a crack so loud that my ears buzzed. This was getting serious.

The guy with the headband held up a newspaper. "Wizard," he cried, jabbing his finger at my picture.

Not that again. "Leave me alone. It's just a game!" Maybe they came from one of those countries that was stuck in the Dark Ages—a place where angry mobs killed anyone they thought was practicing magic. I dropped my hands and took a step back, scanning the walls on either side for any way out. As my right hand brushed my jacket, I got a wild idea.

"Make us," Hurko said.

"Okay, I'll make you," I said. "This will teach you not to mess with a wizard." I grabbed the flash ball I'd gotten from Jenna. With luck, the surprise would give me time to escape. I wanted to shout something that sounded like a magic word. But all my frozen brain could come up with was, "*¡Albóndigas!*"

Hoping that none of them spoke Spanish well enough to realize I'd just shouted, "Meatballs," I closed my eyes against the flash and threw the ball to the ground between me and Hurko. The instant I heard the explosion, I scrambled over the fence.

I glanced back as I dashed away, expecting to see them scurrying after me. But they weren't chasing me. Through the gaps in the fence, I saw all four of them down on one knee, their heads bowed toward the ground, their arms spread wide like little kids playing airplane. They chanted, "Make us!" over and over.

Now that I was free to think about what had happened, my hands started to shake. *You're safe,* I told myself. *You got away.* I calmed down as I walked, but I knew I'd relive that moment in my memory for a long time to come.

When I got near the school, I noticed the picketers hadn't showed up yet. They were probably having a nice, relaxing breakfast somewhere, scarfing down pancakes and building up strength for a long day of marching and shouting. A terrible thought occurred to me. I loved game playing. There was nothing I'd rather do. What if that's how they felt about picketing? What if it was their hobby? Maybe they went to picketing chats, subscribed to picketing magazines, and had online names like *Picketguy* and *SignMaster*. That wouldn't be good.

The bell was just ringing. As I cut over toward the side entrance, a tree ahead of me jerked like it had been hit by an invisible car. Then the leaves started to rustle. It sounded like there was a wrestling match among the branches. Maybe even a tag team match. An instant later, someone dropped to the ground.

"Idiots!" the woman shouted. She glared at the tree, then kicked it. "Stupid tree!" She kicked it again, then turned toward me.

It was the woman from the alley—the older one who'd thrown the rock at me. How'd she get here so fast? I realized she must have run here the back way. But why was she hiding in a tree like a psychotic leopard? Before I could move, she dashed forward and thrust out her hands.

I screamed and leaped back. The woman blinked and stared at me.

"Look. Hurko send gifts. You take." She had half a yo-yo in one hand, the string still wrapped around the exposed axle, and a pair of white plastic doll shoes in the other. "He send gifts as sign of reflect."

"Huh?"

"He have great reflect and agitation for you."

How nice. I had great bewilderment for *her*. "What do you want from me?" I asked, leaving the gifts untouched.

"We want to go home," she said.

"Good idea," I said. "Go home."

"Impossible. There only being four of us. We need being five. Like how we came. With five. Find you, now five wizard again." Her accent was so thick, I had to listen carefully to figure out what she was saying. Maybe that's why her words didn't make any sense.

"I not wizard," I said. Oh crap, I was starting to talk like her. "I'm not a wizard." I spoke slowly and tried to be very clear. Then I repeated the sentence, one word at a time. "*I'M*"—I pointed at myself. "*NOT*"—I shook my head. "*A*"—I clenched my fists. "*WIZARD!*"—I shouted, shooting my hands out and flinging my fingers open like I was casting a spell.

She squealed and flinched as if I was about to hit her. "I beg your forgetness. Not meaning to underworth you." She dropped her head until her chin touched her chest, then raised her gaze but didn't meet my eyes. "You are not just wizard. You are *great* wizard. *Powerful* wizard. You help us. You are magus." A sudden breeze lifted her frizzy hair from her shoulders.

Magus? So that's what they'd been shouting. Not *make us*, but *magus*. I'd seen the word before, but I thought it had a short "a" like in *magic*.

"You are magus," she said again. "Great wizard. Wait.

I remember. Not reflect. Reject. That is word. No wonder so much confusion. Hurko have great reject for your agilities." She grinned like someone who had just aced a tough test.

"Look at me, lady. I'm a kid," I said. The late bell rang. "A kid who should be in class. I have to go." I raced past her with my chin tucked, half expecting I'd get hit in the back of the head by a rock. Behind me, the woman wailed. As I reached the side entrance, something crunched under my foot. A doll shoe. The woman must have thrown it. At least she hadn't pitched another rock. I escaped through the doorway into the school.

"Hey," Jenna said as I dashed into homeroom. "Think up any good uses for the flash balls?"

"A couple," I said. I wondered whether Jenna had any other useful magic in her books at home. I had a funny feeling I was going to need all sorts of help pretty soon.

18

Don't Read Everything You Believe

At lunch, the pretty woman with the long hair slipped up to my table, bowed her head, and dropped an empty thread spool in front of me. It rolled to a stop against my tray. "Gift from Hurko," she said in a voice so quiet, I barely heard her. Then she shouted and started hopping on one foot. Fortunately, the lunchroom was so noisy that you could operate a jackhammer there without attracting attention. She bowed her head again, then dashed out of the cafeteria.

"Who are these people?" I said, staring at the spool.

"What people?" Drew asked.

"Didn't you see her?"

He shook his head. "I didn't see anyone. I was busy watching Dooley." He pointed across the room to where, as far as I could tell, Dooley Cronk was trying to see how many fish sticks he could fit in his mouth without swallowing.

"That kid's going to be famous someday," Drew said. He reached down to pick up his burger. Instead of taking a bite, he dropped it back on his tray, then flipped the bun open and said, "Oh gross."

"What the heck is that?" I asked.

"I think it was lettuce a long time ago," Drew said. He tilted the burger until the shriveled green glob slid off the cheese. It sat on his plate, not quite solid, not quite liquid.

But I was more concerned with weird people than with weird food. "I'll bet they all snuck into the country," I muttered, remembering what Pastor Chuck had said about their accents. "I wish they'd sneak back out."

"Who?" Drew asked.

"These people at the shelter." I handed him my potato chips, since he sure wasn't going to be eating that burger.

"You think so?" Drew seemed interested now. "My dad's got a friend who works for the immigration service over in the city. Want me to tell him? One phone call and they'll swoop down on the place."

"I don't know." I wasn't a snitch. On the other hand, it sure would be nice if those people vanished. I finished my lunch, glad I'd chosen the pizza.

In gym class, while we were running laps, the guy with the headband and sports coat dashed over to me and thrust something heavy into my hands. He shut his eyes, jammed two fingers up his nose, and made that odd screaming sound. Then he ran off.

"What the heck is this?" I asked, looking down at the greasy object he'd left with me.

"A carburetor," Kyle said as he jogged along at my side. "From a Chevy, I think. What was *that* all about?"

"I wish I knew."

"Can I have it?" Kyle asked.

"All yours." I gave him the carburetor and tried to forget about where the guy who'd handed it to me had jammed his fingers.

"What'd you run through?" Kyle asked. He pointed down at my feet.

"I don't know . . ." I stared at my sneakers. They were covered with dust. Thick dust. I stopped and wiped them off with the back of my hand, since my fingers were too greasy, then finished my lap.

By the next period, the picketers had returned, but I hardly noticed them. I was too busy keeping an eye out for Hurko's gang. I got two more gifts in school that day. And three more on the way home, including an old calendar and a bar of chocolate that looked like it had been melted in a fire.

When I got home, I had this crazy urge to raid Dad's toolbox and nail the door shut. Or grab a shovel and dig a moat around the house. I halfway expected to run into one of those lunatics on the way to my room, but I made it there without incident.

First off, I grabbed my dictionary and looked up *magus*.

Yup. It was pronounced with a long "a," so it rhymed with "make us." I'd been wrong about that all my life. Funny how you can assume something is right, maybe for years, and then find out it's not that way at all.

"Magus," I said as I put away the dictionary. However you pronounced it, Hurko had sure picked the wrong guy. Not that I wouldn't *like* to be a real wizard.

I did my homework, then tried to figure out what I was going to say at the school board meeting tomorrow evening. People didn't realize how great games could be at preparing you for life. Everything takes planning and thought. It's just like the real world, except nobody gets hurt when you make a mistake. If people were smart, they'd pass a rule to have games in *every* school.

As I put my homework away, I spotted the book that Pastor Chuck had given me. Why not? He seemed to think it was worth my time. I took it from my backpack and started reading. The whole thing was pretty short. The first part didn't seem to have anything to do with the picketers, but as I got closer to the end, things became interesting. Apparently, the early Christians had argued with each other about all kinds of stuff, including what foods they should and shouldn't eat, and what days were holy. So Paul, who wrote this letter to the Christians in Rome, told them basically to chill out and let each person decide for himself what was right when it came to *disputable matters*. I guess that meant the stuff they were arguing about. He also said they shouldn't judge each other.

"Works for me," I said as I jotted a couple notes. I'd bet those picketers weren't expecting a kid to hit them with an argument right out of the Bible. I wasn't going to back down. So what if they were adults? Being older doesn't automatically make you right. You're in for a battle, Reverend Oakford, I thought as I went to sleep.

In the morning, when I left the house, my mind churned with dozens of arguments. I saw myself giving a stunning speech to the school board. I saw myself convincing them that there was nothing wrong with the convention. I saw them standing to applaud when I was finished. I saw myself . . .

. . . face to face with Hurko and his gang. I was so deep in thought, I hadn't looked where I was going. They were waiting for me on the corner. I'd nearly bumped into them.

I braced myself for the rush of fear I expected to swell up from my guts. But something else came over me instead. Something far more powerful and dangerous than fear.

19

A Little Help

What do you want from me?" I shouted as a wave of anger flooded my body. My fists curled so tight, I felt my nails dig into my palms. I'd put up with enough craziness over the last couple days to last me a lifetime. "What is it? Huh? Why are you bothering me?" I took another step forward. I was right in Hurko's face now, screaming at him. I didn't care. I'd had all I could take. "What the heck do you want?"

Hurko gasped and backed away from me. The others moved with him, as if they were attached by wires. His lip quivered, making his mustache jerk like a caterpillar having a seizure. Tears streamed down his cheeks. My anger was replaced by confusion.

"We want go home," the older woman said. "You help.

Only one. We search so long. Many places. Like finding noodle in haystack. We think we are staying here forever. This seem to be world without magic. Then we sense it. Your power call us to this town. Please, you help us?"

"Do not beg, Nelda," the man with the headband said, grabbing her arm. "We are mightily wizards, too. No wizard should beg."

Nelda yanked her arm free. "I beg if that get us home."

"We are most mightily wizards . . ." the man said. "Our power is awkward and trupendous."

I got the feeling she wanted to kick him like she'd kicked the tree yesterday. Instead, she turned back to me and said, "Please, we need you."

I shook my head. "I don't know what you're talking about. All I know is you've been chasing me, throwing stuff, and screaming." I let out a wail to show them how annoying it was.

They dropped to the ground and covered their heads, as if they expected a bomb to explode. For an instant, I wondered if I'd actually hit them with some sort of spell. But there'd been no sign of any magic. No flash, no boom, no shaking of the earth. Even so, the four of them didn't look like they planned to move anytime soon.

"Hey—knock that off," I said. "Get up."

Hurko peeked at me from between the arms he'd wrapped around his head.

"I won't hurt you," I said.

He got slowly to his feet, followed by the others. "Help us, Magus," he said.

"Please," Nelda said, staring at me with moist eyes.

I have to get away from these wackos, I thought. But then I heard a different voice in my mind. Michelle. What was it she'd said the other day? *I think it's the people we don't want to be around who need our help the most.* Crap. Why did I have to be stuck with such a good memory?

"Look, if I promise to try to help you, will you stop following me?" I asked Hurko.

He nodded.

I had no idea how I could help, but I knew I couldn't deal with this by running away. "I have an important meeting at the school board tonight. After that, I'll see what I can do. Okay?"

"Yes. Thank you," Hurko said.

"Thank you, Magus," Nelda said.

The young woman added her thanks in a quiet voice. The other man grumbled something. They backed away, tossing a couple more thank-yous in my direction as they left.

I waited until they'd turned the corner, then headed for school. Man. What in the world did they think I could do? I had to make them understand that I wasn't a real wizard. Not that it mattered. Whatever help they needed—it wasn't magic.

Still, I couldn't keep from thinking how great it would be to cast spells. I stopped walking, checked to make sure nobody was in sight, then wailed and slapped my cheek like that woman had done. Nothing happened, except my cheek hurt. A lot. "Get real, Mercer," I muttered to myself as I continued toward school.

I had to slip past the picketers. I guess they'd come early to get their enthusiasm up for tonight's meeting. Well, I had my enthusiasm up, too. During the day, I checked with every game player I knew, and they all promised to come. This was our school. There was no way we'd let a bunch of outsiders tell us what to do.

That evening, I was too nervous to eat much dinner. My parents were coming to the meeting, but I didn't want to wait for them, so I went ahead on my own.

The board meets in the town hall. I got there early enough to be the first one in the room. There was a table up front with seven chairs behind it. A bunch more chairs faced the table. I'd brought all my notes, and the book Pastor Chuck had given me. Man, it was really going to stop Reverend Oakford cold when I smacked him with some lines from Romans. I was all set for combat.

I could hear the Game Lord describing the scenario. *You are in a chamber, facing a tribe of ogres. Their leader carries a large, leather-bound book. He screams at you in fury. What do you do?*

I paced for a while, then sat down and thought about my

battle plans. Ten minutes before the meeting, people started to drift in. Some of them—board members, I guess—took seats at the table up front.

I was pleasantly surprised when Michelle sat down in the seat to my right. "Ready?" she asked.

"I hope so."

"I'm ready," Jenna said, dropping into the chair on my left. She was wearing a regular shirt and jeans for a change, but she hadn't left the house looking completely normal. She pointed to a large green stone that dangled from a chain around her neck. "This is the most effective crystal for persuasion. I made up some candles, too, but I don't know if they'll let me burn them here." She set a paper bag down on the floor by her feet.

"Probably not," I said, glad that at least she hadn't decided to come dressed in witch's clothes.

Ed slipped into a seat one row behind me and flipped open a notebook. "You here to measure my horns?" I asked.

"I'm just here to report the truth," he said, pulling a pen from his pocket.

I thought about the reporter from the *Cryer*. Unlike Ed, she'd taken the time to examine both sides of the story. "You'll never know the truth," I said. "You've already made up your mind. You didn't even bother to watch us play the game."

"It wasn't necessary," he said. "I knew what it was about."

"You don't know anything." I turned away from him and checked out the other end of the front row. Reverend Oakford was there, along with a couple dozen people. They were standing in a circle, holding hands and praying.

"Can they do that at a board meeting?" Michelle asked.

"If they keep it up, I'm going to start chanting," Jenna said.

Fortunately, she didn't get a chance.

"All righty," a man sitting in the middle seat at the table said. I recognized him from town. It was Mr. Parma, who owned the dry cleaning shop. "Let's get this meeting started."

20

Disorderly Conduct

I figured I'd get to discuss the tournament right away. But the meeting didn't work like that. First, one person read some notes telling what had happened at the last meeting. Then a bunch of people reported about different projects. Next, they spent half an hour discussing whether to build a new snack shed for the football field. I learned more about the art of making large quantities of nachos than I'd ever wanted to know.

Finally, Mr. Parma scanned the crowd and asked, "Any new business?" He pointed at Mr. Abruzzi, who had raised his hand.

Mr. Abruzzi stood up and said, "The students at Oscar Wilde Middle School would like to discuss the fund-raiser. Apparently, there are some causes for concern, and the administration feels that the board should be involved. I'll let the kids speak for themselves."

Before Mr. Abruzzi could even sit back down, Reverend Oakford sprang to his feet.

"I demand to be heard," he shouted.

Mr. Parma rocked back a bit in his chair and stared for a moment. But then he told the reverend to go ahead.

Reverend Oakford cleared his throat with a sound like a revving motorcycle, then stomped to the front of the room. "It has come to my attention that there is a dangerous and deadly enemy prowling the halls of our schools. Our children are at risk!"

He stressed the end of each sentence in a weird way, so *risk* became *riskuh*, and *schools* became *schoolszuh*. It made him sound sort of like he had an angry Swedish accent.

"They are consorting with demons, devils, and witches," the reverend said. He glared at Jenna. I squirmed in the reflected shower of hatred, but Jenna smiled back at him and waved. He flipped his Bible open and read, "Thou shall not suffer a witch to live!"

"Whoa—time out!" Mr. Parma said. "Sir, this is a public meeting. As you well know, our federal constitution doesn't permit religious arguments at government functions. You can speak all you want, but you can't read from the Bible."

"I follow the word of God, not the word of man," the reverend shouted.

Several members of his group yelled, "Amen!"

"You can't talk about God, either," Mr. Parma told him. "That's not my personal belief. It's the law. Keeping this in mind, do you have anything else to say?"

"I have a great deal more," the reverend said, snapping his Bible shut with a bang. "This school—this institution for learning—permits children to dabble with the devil and delve into the occult."

He raged on, pacing as he talked, making us sound like a tribe of evil creatures who danced around a fire while summoning demons. Jeez—all we did was roll dice and have fun.

On my left, Jenna muttered comments about everything the reverend said. "You know what a witch is?" she asked. "Do you know who they mean by *witch*?"

"A sorcerer?" I guessed, trying to answer her and listen to the reverend at the same time.

"Anyone who's different," she said. "That's who they mean. Anyone who dares to think differently, or even look different. Anyone who doesn't fit into the neat little box of their beliefs. Me. You. Galileo. Probably Einstein and Ben Franklin for that matter. That's who they mean. Sick people, too. People who hear voices. People who need help."

She stopped to catch her breath, then switched topics. "You know what punishment the Bible gives for kids who talk back to their parents?"

"You get sent to your tent with no television?" I guessed.

"Not even close," Jenna said. "You get stoned to death."

Wow—if kids these days got killed for talking back, that would be the end of the human race. "Look," I whispered, "I don't care what they believe. I just want them to leave me alone."

"It doesn't work that way," Jenna said. "They care what *you* believe."

"How do you know so much about the Bible anyhow?" I asked.

"When I was little, I wanted to be a nun," she said.

I couldn't tell whether she was joking. But, knowing the way she hopped from one interest to another, it wouldn't surprise me at all.

Finally, amazingly, Reverend Oakford pulled a handkerchief from his pocket, mopped the stream of sweat that was flowing down his forehead, closed his mouth, and plopped back in his chair. As the reverend sat, one of the men in his group shouted, "Hallelujah!"

Mr. Parma sighed, then asked, "Is there anyone else who'd like to speak on this issue?"

Jenna raised her hand. I kicked her bag hard, spilling the candles across the floor. As she scurried to pick them up, I stood and raised my hand.

"Go ahead, young man," Mr. Parma said.

It was strange. I was sure I'd be nervous. But the moment I started to speak, I felt calm. "I'm Mercer Dickensen. I'm in the eighth grade at Oscar Wilde." I added the part about my school to let them know I wasn't an outsider. Then

I launched into my attack. "For starters, I'm surprised any-one would object to what we're doing. Especially anyone who reads the Bible," I said, staring at the reverend.

He stared back at me, but his smug expression flickered briefly into the puzzled face of someone who's just seen the road ahead make an unexpected turn. I opened the book to the first spot where I'd stuck a Post-it note. This was going to be great. "If you look at Romans in chapter fourteen—"

"Now hold it, son," Mr. Parma said. "You can't read from the Bible. I thought I already explained that."

"But this isn't stuff against the tournament," I said. "It's against forcing your beliefs on other people."

He held up his hand. "Doesn't make a difference, son. For, against, or sideways for that matter, you can't read from the Bible at a school board meeting. You just can't. Under-stand?"

"But—"

"No exceptions," he said. "If you've got a problem with that, you'll have to take it up with the Supreme Court."

That killed my whole strategy. I'd planned to thump the reverend with his own weapon, then slam him with a bunch of other arguments. I felt like my bowstring had snapped on the first pull, before the battle had even started.

"Anything else to say?" Mr. Parma asked.

"Sure. Lots." Where to start? All my neatly stacked ar-guments had collapsed into a jumbled mess in my mind. As I pulled my thoughts together, I saw a new attack. "The whole complaint against Wizards of the Warrior World is based on religion. So they can't even use it here," I said.

"That game *is* a religion!" the reverend shouted. He leaped out of his seat and aimed a quivering finger at me. "It's a worship of darkness and a celebration of evil."

Before I could answer, other voices joined the argument, shouting out from all over the room.

"Save our children," a woman behind me yelled.

"Let the kids have their fun," a man shouted back.

"It's demon worship, that's what it is!"

"This is crazy. It's just a game."

"School ain't no place for games. Get back to reading and writing."

"Judge not, lest you be judged."

That last one came from Jenna. "Figured I could sneak in some Scripture," she said, grinning at me.

"ORDER!" Mr. Parma yelled, slamming his palm on the table. "Let's have some order in here."

That didn't do much good. People screamed and hollered. I think a fistfight might have broken out in the back of the room, but it was too noisy to tell for sure. It was like a Little League game right after a bad call at the plate.

While the arguments raged, Mr. Parma huddled with the other board members. When things calmed down to the point where he could be heard, he said, "All right, let's get back to order here. This is a meeting, not a rodeo."

I started to get up, figuring he'd let me finish my side of

the argument. Reverend Oakford had talked a whole bunch, and then he'd interrupted me before I'd even had my turn. It would only be fair for me to get my chance now.

I froze as I heard Mr. Parma's next words.

"The board has made its decision."

21

Hit by a Board

I tried to prepare myself for the worst. Across the room, Reverend Oakford bowed his head and clenched his fists.

"The students mean no harm," Mr. Parma said. "And the fund-raiser is a middle-school tradition."

I realized my own fists were clenched. I took a slow breath and relaxed my fingers.

"We cannot let religion enter into the decision," he said.

"All right," Jenna said. "Score one for the home team."

I glanced over my shoulder and smirked at Ed. Victory was so sweet.

"But there's obviously a moral problem here that goes beyond issues of religion," Mr. Parma said. "The convention, with its focus on demons and sorcery, has upset a lot of people. Too many questions have been raised. We can't allow the school to sanction this event. The students will just have to find another way to raise money."

He might as well have thrust a sword through my heart.

The reverend leaped up and shouted, "Hallelujah!" He raced to the table, where he started shaking hands. "Praise the Lord! I knew you were God-fearing people."

"That does it," Jenna said, snatching up her bag of candles. "I'm going to sue someone. That's what I'll do. No, I'm going to hex someone. That'll teach 'em."

"Now what?" Michelle asked as Jenna stomped out of the room.

"I don't know," I said. "It's over, I guess."

"There has to be something we can do," she said.

"Maybe we should have a meeting," I told her. Then, despite the emptiness I felt, or maybe because of it, I laughed.

"What's so funny?" she asked.

"Meetings," I said, looking around the room where a dozen arguments had broken out. "That's the problem, not the solution. But I guess you're right—we have to try to figure out what to do. Why don't we get together during study hall tomorrow?"

"Good idea." She put a hand on my arm. "Sorry they voted against us."

I nodded, not trusting my voice.

When Michelle left, I turned to Ed, who was still sitting behind me. "I hope your church has a lot of money for the

Sharing Shepherd," I said. "Because they aren't getting any from our school. Thanks to you."

I didn't stick around to listen to his excuses. I found my folks and told them I'd rather walk home. They understood. Then I pushed my way through the crowd. It was over. No convention. I'd lost. We'd all lost.

What else can go wrong? I wondered as I headed outside. The answer was waiting for me on the sidewalk.

"It is after meeting," Hurko said, gazing at me with the expectant look of a three-year-old who's been promised a trip to the toy store.

"Right. Yeah. It's after the meeting," I said. I needed to get away from him. I needed to get away from everyone.

"You will help us now?" Nelda asked.

"Look," I said, "something I really cared about just got snatched away from me. Do you have any clue what that feels like?"

Nelda stared back at me as if I'd just asked the world's dumbest question. Which I guess I had.

I pointed to the lawn in front of the elementary school. "Let's go over there," I said. "The place is quiet, and we can talk." It was time to explain that there were no eighth-grade sorcerers of the sort they needed.

They followed me across the street. "I'm not a great wizard," I told them.

"You are too . . ." Hurko paused, as if searching for a word. Then his face lit up and he said, "Moddish."

Nelda moved her hand through the air as if stroking a piece of silk. "We feel your greatness. It flow through whole town. Like big, starving river. There is power here."

"We have power, too, Nelda," the guy with the headband said.

She turned toward him and said, "Brag, brag, brag. Your words will not take us home." She looked back at me. "But stupid Tortwaller is right. We have muchness of powers." She pointed to the younger woman. "Do you know what Zee can do?"

"What?" I asked.

"She can turn brindlewood into gold," Nelda said.

"I've never heard of brindlewood," I said.

"There is reasoning for that. No brindlewood on this stupid world," Nelda said. "That why you never hear of it."

Now I understood. They really *were* crazy. They thought they were wizards, but they had an explanation for why they couldn't do any magic. They didn't need me. They needed real help.

Nelda kept talking about the other woman. "Zee know many spells. Show him, Zee. Show Magus how you make plants wilt."

"He does not want to see," Zee whispered. She shoved her hands into the pockets of her overalls.

"Show him," Tortwaller said. He stared at me. "Give this *magus* a detonation of your power."

"You want?" Zee asked.

"Yeah, right. Sure," I said, wishing I was anywhere else but there. "Wilt some plants for me."

She gazed at the ground by my feet and let out one of those weird screams, then hopped from foot to foot. With her long hair bouncing around, she looked like a little kid skipping rope.

The grass rippled. I knelt for a closer look. Every blade in an area about a foot across had flopped over. As I watched, the grass melted into an oozing liquid. I stood up and backed away from the spot. What was going on? Maybe she'd sprayed it with some kind of weed killer.

"I have also power," Tortwaller said. He let out a little scream and jammed his fingers up his nose.

I remembered his performance in my gym class. Half afraid to look, I glanced down at my sneakers. They were covered with dust. Oh man—this was real.

"That just top of iceworm," Tortwaller said. "I do much more. I make animal talk." He pointed at a squirrel, let out a small scream, then reached in his mouth and grabbed his tongue.

That would be awesome, I thought. My mind filled with a dozen great ways to use the spell.

The squirrel twitched its tail and said, "Pretzel thermometer." It hopped a couple feet closer, said, "Chewing lazy igloo zipper," then dashed up a tree. All things considered, it made just about as much sense as Tortwaller.

"I bend metal," Hurko said. "I try show you in kitchen.

Bend knife. But you too busy staring at girl. Not caring what I do."

"And I move things," Nelda said. She grabbed a stone from the ground, squeezed it, and let out a scream. As she slapped her cheek with her empty hand, the stone shot from her grip, sailed across the lawn, and bounced off a stop sign with a clang.

"We are most mightily together," Tortwaller said. "Behold."

They formed a circle, linked hands, and let out a joint scream. Then they all kicked one leg to the side, like a group of off-balance Irish dancers.

I heard a hiss—the kind you get when you open a vacuum-sealed jar of peanuts. I guess it was air rushing in to fill up the empty space. Nelda was gone.

22

FOR MY NEXT TRICK...

What happened to her?" I asked.

"Nelda is safety," Hurko told me. "We send her across street."

"No you did not!" The muffled shout came from a maple tree to my left. The leaves rustled and then Nelda's feet appeared, swinging back and forth as she dangled from a low branch. She dropped the remaining yard to the ground and clomped back over to us. "Every time. Why you send me into tree? If was one tree on whole stupid world, you send me into it. If no trees on world, you plant tree just so you send me there."

"Too much complain. You short. Tree tall. Be happy for nice view," Tortwaller said.

Nelda glared at him, then turned to me. "You see? Always a sewer puss."

"Uh-huh," I said after I'd managed to get my jaw working. Wizards, I thought. They were *real* wizards. Not pretend game wizards, but real, honest to goodness, flesh and blood wizards who could cast spells. Real magic. Wow.

"Please help us," Zee said.

"I'll do whatever I can." Everything had been turned sideways. All the magic that lived in my imagination had suddenly become possible. Wizards. Amazing. "What do you need?"

"Five wizards to cross worlds," Nelda said, stretching her arms wide. "Our world." She wiggled the fingers of her left hand. "Your world." She shook her head. "Not same place."

I nodded, numbly, as the idea sank in. I'd read enough fantasy stories, so I understood what she meant. Other worlds—other realities—completely separate from ours. Not somewhere else in our universe—somewhere else entirely. You couldn't get there from here no matter how far you traveled.

"We see poster." Nelda pulled a ragged piece of cloth from a pocket in her skirt. "I still have," she said, holding it up.

The writing was just dots and squiggles. "I can't read that," I told her.

"Stupid me," Nelda said. "You do not know Gliphidetsian. I read for you. Wait, better yet," she said, turning toward Tortwaller. "Do word spell."

He stared at the cloth, let out a little scream, and crossed his eyes. Then Nelda screamed as the cloth flapped violently in her hand and turned into a bat. She flung it away and it headed for the trees. Just before it flew out of sight, I heard it say, "Noodle shoe jiggle tower."

"Wrong spell, stupid," Nelda told Tortwaller.

"Because I know so many," he said. "Not like you."

Nelda turned back to me. "I tell Magus what poster said. Have big adventure. See many worlds. We find, too late, wizard in charge want steal from other worlds."

"That doesn't sound too good," I said.

"Terrible trip," Hurko said. "First world, all ice."

"Next world even worse," Nelda said. She shuddered. "Horrible creatures live there. Mobsters."

"Monsters?" I asked.

"Yes. Bad monsters," Hurko said. He pulled down the neck of his shirt, revealing a jagged scar that ran across his collarbone.

"Next we find this stupid world," Nelda said.

"What happened to the other wizard?" I asked.

"We land in middle of zoo," Nelda said. "Nighttime. There is creature on our world called pawnula. Big, but very gentle. Easy to ride."

"Large paws, whiskers, and stripes," Hurko said. "White and orange stripes. Long tail, wave all the time." He made a motion with his hand.

"Sounds like a tiger," I said.

(121)

"Look like tiger," Nelda told me.

"He tried to ride one?" I asked.

She nodded. "He climb into cage." Nelda flinched. "He never climb out."

"Cat food," Tortwaller said.

"We cannot go home," Hurko said. "We are strangled here."

"Unless we find wizard," Nelda said.

"But I'm not . . ."

They stared at me with so much hope.

". . . sure if I know the best way to send you home." There had to be something I could do. I'd been training my whole life for this. I knew all about magic. So did my friends. "I have a meeting tomorrow, with the best wizards around here. I'll see if we can think of a way to help."

"Be careful who you tell," Nelda said. "Some worlds, wizards hunted down. This is world like that, I think."

"I'll be careful," I told her. I could just imagine the panic if word got around. It was bad enough seeing what happened to game-playing wizards. "It's a small meeting."

"Meetings," Tortwaller said. "Always meetings. Crazy world."

"Yeah," I said, nodding. "Always meetings." But tomorrow's meeting was going to be a big surprise for everyone.

23

The Tables Are
(Re)turned

I had my own surprise when I got to study hall the next day. The room was half empty. "Where is everyone?" I asked Kyle.

"Some of the kids got in trouble," he said. "Their parents don't want them to play any more because of all the bad stuff they heard at the school board. Kenny told me he had to drop out of the game sessions. So did Brian and Natalie."

"That stinks," I said. I glanced at Drew's empty chair, hoping he was just late.

"Drew's folks took away his dice. Can you believe that?" Kyle said.

"Believe what?" Michelle asked as she joined us.

"A bunch of parents are all freaked out," I said.

"We have to fight this," Jenna said. "If we give up, they've won. And that would mean we've lost."

Michelle nodded. "Absolutely. We can't give up. This is about more than the game. It's about our rights. Just because we're kids, people treat us as if we don't have rights."

I nearly gave my head a hard shake. Michelle sounded like Jenna. Next thing I knew, Jenna would be teaching Michelle how to tell fortunes. Or Michelle would teach Jenna how to shoot baskets.

They all started talking about their rights. But I had something just as important to tell them. "You're not going to believe this," I said.

Before I could say any more, the door opened and Donny came into the room. He didn't look happy.

"Something's going on," Kyle said.

Donny spoke with the teacher for a moment, then went from table to table, talking to the kids. At each stop, I could see heads droop and shoulders sag. Donny was carrying bad news.

"What's up?" I asked him when he reached us.

"Principal wants the tables out," he said. "No games in school."

"No games!" I said. "Ever?"

Donny shrugged. "Don't know. At least not until the next parents' meeting."

"That sucks," I said.

"Sorry. Nothing I can do. Now me, I think you kids are great. No harm in your game. The world needs a little magic now and then. But I don't make the rules."

We stood aside as he folded up the table. Where does it stop? I wondered. No convention. No games in school. Then what? No games at home?

"What are we going to do?" Kyle asked after Donny had hauled out the last table.

"Protest," Jenna said. "We'll go on a hunger strike. Or have a sit-in."

"Let's start a petition," Michelle said.

None of that sounded like it would help. But at least I could tell them about the magic that nobody could take away from us. "I found some real wizards," I said.

"Maybe we could get a lawyer," Kyle said.

"Too expensive," Michelle told him. "They charge like a hundred dollars an hour."

"I found some real wizards," I said again.

"I still think a protest would be the best idea," Jenna said. "We could chain ourselves together."

"I could make signs," Kyle said. "And we could all sit here until they let us play."

"I found some real wizards," I said a third time.

"But a protest—" Michelle's head snapped in my direction. "What did you say, Mercer?"

"I found some real wizards."

"Very funny," Kyle said.

"I'm serious." I told them everything that had happened. It helped that they'd already witnessed some of the magic. Michelle had seen Hurko bend a knife, and Kyle had seen Tortwaller cover my sneakers with dust. Only, at the time, we didn't know it was magic.

Jenna didn't need to be convinced. If I'd told her I was in touch with the spirit of George Washington, she wouldn't have blinked. She'd probably just ask for his autograph. But there was one part of my story she questioned. "How come they came to you? Why not me?"

"They felt my power," I said. I didn't want to brag, but it was the truth.

Jenna shook her head. "You said they felt power in town. All around town. It could just as easily be coming from me. Right?"

There was no point arguing with her. Once she latched on to a position, she wouldn't let go until she'd won. "Right," I said. "It could be from anyone. The important thing is that these people are real wizards."

"This is perfect!" Jenna said. "They can help us win the fight. We can blow away our enemies with magic."

"Hardly." Sending Reverend Oakford into a tree wouldn't solve our problems. I thought about dusty feet and wilted plants. As exciting as it was to meet wizards, I couldn't fool myself about the usefulness of their spells. It was *we* who had to help *them*. "Any ideas how to get them back to their world?" I asked.

"Sure. No problem," Jenna said.

"No problem?" I asked.

She nodded. "I've got all kinds of real spells at home."

Yesterday morning, I wouldn't have paid any attention to her. But yesterday morning, I hadn't yet come face-to-face with my own private magic show. "So what do we need to do?" I asked.

"We just have to open a transdimensional gate to their world. Probably with a portal spell."

"Oh, is that all?" I asked.

"That's all." She closed her eyes for a moment, as if seeing a page in her mind. "We'll need moss from a black walnut tree. I remember that part. I think the spell uses ginseng, too. I'll have to check on the rest of the ingredients. And we'll need a fire for the ceremony. The hotter the better. Oh, and a full moon. Anyone know when the moon's going to be full?"

"Next full moon is tonight," a voice behind me said.

It belonged to Ed.

24

Playing With the Truth

Oh great. "How long have you been listening?" I asked Ed.

"Just got here. Heard Jenna mention the full moon. Look, I've been thinking about what you said. You're right. A good writer doesn't assume anything. I can't know the truth without seeing both sides for myself."

"What's the point now?" I asked. "You've won. You got what you wanted."

"I didn't want the shelter to lose out," Ed said. "Maybe I can fix that. I can write another article. People listen to what I write. You've seen that."

"They listened once," I said. "That doesn't mean they'll listen again. Besides, you've already decided the game is bad."

"If you think I'm wrong, give me a chance to find out the truth." Ed glanced past me at the empty space where the table had been. "You guys playing on the floor now?"

"No, we're not playing on the floor," I said. "It seems there've been some objections to us playing at all. I wonder how that could have happened?"

Ed and I stared at each other. It was Michelle who broke the silence. "So let's play," she said, pushing a chair back and dropping to the floor. She looked up at us. "I'd still rather watch, but why don't the four of you play?"

"Sounds like a plan," Kyle said. He plopped down across from her.

I glanced toward the front of the room, where the teacher was reading a magazine, then joined Michelle on the floor. I halfway expected the teacher to say something. Heck, I halfway expected sirens to go off and Reverend Oakford to burst through the door. But the teacher didn't even look up, and I guess Reverend Oakford and his vanful of picketers were on their way to their next battle.

Ed sat with us. I explained the basic rules and told him how to select a character. "Can I be a minister?" he asked.

"There's no such role," I said. "There are priests."

Ed shook his head. "I want to be a minister. Can't I make up a role?"

"Sure," Kyle said.

So Ed became the first minister ever to walk the face of Zule. When he'd set up his character, he spent all his money on food and clothing. He didn't get any armor. And he forgot to buy a weapon. I wanted to warn him, but that would be against the rules. He'd just have to figure it out for himself.

With a nervous glance to the front of the room, we started playing.

Jenna grinned when her turn came. "I hurl my spear," she said, looking straight at Ed.

Not again, I thought, picturing the shaft shooting through the defenseless minister, pinning him to a wall like a butterfly in a museum. Minister to martyr in one easy step. This sure wasn't going to help win Ed over to our side.

"I hurl my spear into the ground at the feet of this weaponless stranger, offering it to him as a gift," Jenna said. "I welcome him to our world."

On his next turn, Ed accepted the gift. Then he brought the spear to town and sold it. He used the money to buy food for the poor. After that, he crossed the river and headed toward a village that had been struck with a plague. He didn't get far. His path through the mountain pass was blocked by a giant boulder.

An experienced adventurer wouldn't have had any problem. But Ed was new at this. He spent the rest of his turns trying a bunch of things that didn't work. Before he could figure out a way around the boulder, the period ended.

"So what do you think?" I asked him.

Ed took a deep breath. I expected to get a lecture about demons and sorcery. But all he said was, "It's a game."

"That's what I've been trying to tell you," I said.

"It was even kind of fun," he admitted. "Not that I'd

want to play it again or anything. But I can see where it's fun for other people."

"Just a game friends play," Michelle said. "That's all I see here. If they thought it was real, they wouldn't call it *fantasy* role-playing."

"Guess not. I should have played it before I wrote that column." Ed paused, then said, "You gotta admit, it was a pretty powerful piece of writing."

"Yeah. It was." I felt bad for him. "You're definitely a good writer."

"Thanks." He got up and headed off.

As we gathered our gaming gear, Jenna took over again. "I'll know more after I check my books," she said. "But let's plan to do the spell tonight. Otherwise, we'll have to wait until next month. Kyle, you get the moss. Okay? There are some black walnut trees down by the pond. Mercer, you need to tell the wizards to be ready. Michelle, can you buy some ginseng at the health food store?"

We all nodded. I held up Shath'dra and said, "You can bring the donuts," then put him in my backpack and zipped it up.

"This is going to be great," Jenna said as she dashed out.

I turned to Michelle. "I hope it's not a mistake letting her pick the spell."

"You don't believe it'll work?" Michelle asked.

I shrugged. "Who knows? A couple days ago, I didn't even believe in wizards."

25

Vanishing Wizards

All the way to the Sharing Shepherd, I kept expecting the wizards to pop up somewhere. They didn't. They weren't inside the shelter, either.

But Pastor Chuck was there, peeling potatoes. "Hey, my favorite volunteer." He grinned at me, and then looked over at a stack of pots and pans.

I sighed and went to the sink. Great. Tuna casserole. Or the remains of it. As I washed the pots, I kept checking through the double doors. No sign of Hurko, but plenty of other folks filled the shelter. "All the fuss about the convention," I said, "and that's who's getting hurt." I pointed a wet hand toward the front room.

Pastor Chuck nodded. "That's the way it usually turns out. The people who start a battle rarely see the victims."

"I don't understand why they're picking on us. And it's

not just the demon thing. It's like they hate every part of the game." I glanced at my backpack, where I'd stashed all my gaming gear. "What's the big deal about dice, anyhow?" I asked.

Pastor Chuck tilted his head toward the shelf and said, "Check out John, chapter nineteen, verses twenty-three and twenty-four."

I dried my hands, opened the Bible, and read about how the soldiers had cast lots to see who would get Jesus' coat.

"So they used dice?"

"Not exactly, but close," Pastor Chuck said. "They threw something. Probably some kind of stones."

"Is that why some people get so weird about dice?" I asked.

He nodded. Then he smiled and said, "Now read Acts, chapter one, verse twenty-six."

"Are you trying to trick me into reading the Bible?" I asked.

"Heaven forbid. Trust me, just read the verse."

I found Acts, which was right next to John, and read the part where the disciples picked someone to replace Judas. They made their choice by casting lots. "Now the good guys are doing it, right?"

"You betcha," Pastor Chuck said.

"So what's it all mean?" I asked.

"It means nobody should use one small passage from the Bible to decide important issues. Anyone can take an isolated verse and warp it to fit his own use. That's how cults get started. We could talk for hours about that stuff. People think games are scary? They should worry about the madness that goes on in the real world."

He sighed and shook his head. "You don't get anywhere by screaming at people. The basic message is pretty simple. You'll find some version of the Golden Rule in just about every religion on the planet. Treat people the way you want them to treat you. You like that better than, 'Don't touch those dice'?"

"Sounds pretty reasonable." It almost seemed as though Pastor Chuck and Reverend Oakford came from entirely different worlds, too.

I hurried to finish the pots. As much as I liked hanging out with Pastor Chuck, I needed to find the wizards. "By the way," I asked, trying to make it sound like a casual question, "where's that guy? You know. Hurko. Is he around?"

Pastor Chuck shook his head. "He and his friends got scared off when they saw the men from Immigration."

"What?" My stomach squeezed into a tight ball. I remembered Drew telling me about his dad's friend. *One phone call, and they'll swoop down on the place.* Drew must have made that call, thanks to me and my big mouth.

"They come by here once in a while, looking for illegal aliens. Haven't been around in a long time. Guess they got a tip or something. They take suspects to the local police station."

"Would they take Hurko?" I asked.

"What do you think?"

"I guess, with that accent, they might wonder where he's from," I said.

Pastor Chuck nodded. "On top of that, Hurko doesn't have any proof that he's a citizen. None of them has any identification at all, for that matter."

"What happens if they get caught?" I asked.

"I guess they'll get sent back to wherever they came from," Pastor Chuck said.

Good luck with that, I thought.

"Hey—don't look so worried," he said. "They'll show up in a couple days. They're survivors. As strange as they act, they've managed to look out for each other so far."

"Yeah, I guess." I stacked the last of the pots on the drain board, then headed to the nearest phone to call Jenna.

"I got it all under control," she said. "Found the perfect portal spell. I even know where to get the fire we need. We can use the kiln in the art room. It's still open at night, right?"

"Probably. But there's a problem." I explained that the wizards were missing.

"You're just going to have to find them," Jenna said. "I've done all this work. I'm not letting it go to waste. Find them, and meet me at the school around eight-thirty. I already got in touch with Kyle and Michelle. We'll see you there."

"But . . ."

She hung up.

I called Mom and asked if I could skip dinner. I told her I was doing something with Kyle. That was true enough. Mom said it was okay.

I searched all around town, trying to figure out where Hurko and his group would go if they couldn't stay at the shelter. By the time it started to get dark, I was ready to give up. I'd checked every place I could think of. There had to be somewhere they felt safe. Somewhere they'd go when they couldn't go anywhere else.

Oh no. I remembered a quote I'd read in English class. Where do you go when you can't go anyplace else? Home. That's where you go. They didn't have a home. Not in this universe. But I did.

As I raced toward my house, images flashed through my mind of Hurko and the gang knocking at my door and asking my mom, Can Mercer come out and play?

26

Look Who Popped Up

I dashed through my front door. Nobody was in the living room. Then I heard Mom's voice. "This is just so hard to believe," she said.

I ran toward the kitchen.

"It's not possible," she said. "It's just not possible."

I reached the kitchen and slid halfway across the floor.

Mom looked calmly at me from her seat on a stool next to the counter. She had a mug of tea in one hand, and the phone in the other. "Hold on, Maggie," she said. She put down the tea, placed her palm over the mouthpiece, and said, "Something wrong?"

Oops. No wizards in sight. Just Mom talking on the phone with her friend.

"No, everything's okay," I said. "Anybody stop by?"

She shook her head. "Expecting someone?"

"Not really." I headed up to my room to try to figure out my next move. Before I could even flip on the light, I heard a tapping.

That's when I saw the face outside my window.

"Whoa!" I shouted, jumping back.

"What was that, Mercer?" Mom called from downstairs.

"Nothing," I called back. I closed my door and rushed over to the window. Nelda was hovering outside. Wow—if she could float, that was a pretty awesome spell. Floating was almost as good as flying. Maybe they *were* powerful wizards after all. Then I looked down. Nelda was standing on Zee's shoulders. And Zee was standing on Tortwaller's back as he knelt on all fours.

"Imitation cops get Hurko," Nelda said. "We go bust him loose."

Nelda started to fall away from the window as Zee staggered. I grabbed her arm and helped her inside.

"Thank you," she said. Then her eyes found the lava demon. She was a bit less cool about it than Ed had been. She let out a scream. For a small person, she had a lot of lung power.

"Sssshhh," I said. Too late. Even as I spoke, I could hear Mom racing up the stairs.

I ran to the door and stuck my head out. No way I wanted to explain why I had a stranger in my room. Especially not a strange adult female wizard.

"What's wrong?" Mom asked, her eyes wide with concern.

"New game," I said. "Computer game. Screaming Mummy Ghost Ghouls. Great graphics. The rotting flesh effects are awesome. Want to play? I'm just about to see if an ax works against a giant worm." I grabbed an imaginary ax handle, swung my fists, and made squishing noises.

"No, thanks. I'll pass. But turn the volume down. All right?"

"Absolutely." I closed the door. Across the room, Nelda was still staring at the demon.

"It's not real," I said. "It's just a statue."

She edged closer and poked the lava demon in the chest with one finger, then jumped away as it rocked back and forth. When it had settled, she dashed forward, said, "Stupid statue," and punched it. The statue bounced off the wall and one of its horns went flying.

"Feel better?" I asked.

"Much," she said.

"Tell me what happened," I said. "But tell me quietly."

"We all leave when we see Imitation cops. But Hurko forget hat. Stupid hat. He think he is cowboy. He sneak back for hat. They catch him. Take him away."

"Oh boy. He'll be at the police station. We have to get him out." Then I told her about Jenna's plan.

"I have idea," she said. "Zee can make their plants wilt. They run in terror. We free Hurko."

"Yeah . . . we'll do something like that." I hoped we could come up with a better plan. But first, we had to get there. "Look, can you go back through the window? I'll meet you by the side of the house."

Nelda crawled onto Zee's shoulders. Then she climbed down the human ladder. After I'd closed my window, I looked around the room in search of an excuse to go out. And there it was, right in front of me.

"Perfect." I shoved the broken horn in my backpack, then grabbed the lava demon and carried it downstairs. "The art room's open late tonight," I said to Mom. "Okay if I fix this?"

"As long as you don't stay out too late," Mom said. "It's a school night. Do you need some help with that thing?"

"No, I'm fine. Thanks."

I joined the three wizards on the lawn. Zee seemed happy to see me, though she gave the lava demon a nervous look. I tapped the statue to show her it was hollow and harmless. Meanwhile, Tortwaller stood off by himself and glared.

"What's his problem?" I asked Nelda.

"His power not great in this world," she said. "Make him feel worthless."

"That's no excuse for being such a grump," I said.

Nelda nodded. "You telling me? I listen to Tortwaller all day."

"Well, if we're lucky, you'll be home soon." Lugging the lava demon, and leading a pack of wizards, I headed for the police station. When we got there, I didn't have any idea what to do. I couldn't just ask them to let Hurko go. *Excuse me, Officer, would you mind releasing that illegal alien into my custody?* Right. That would work. Maybe I could run up to him and shout, "Uncle Hurko, we've been looking all over for you!"

At least I knew where to look. In the fifth grade, we'd taken a class trip to the police station. The teachers had herded us down a hall to the back of the place, locked us up in cells, and explained that this was what life would be like if we didn't do our homework.

I led the wizards around the building. As we reached the rear wall, I heard a cry of, "Magus!"

Hurko waved at us from behind the bars of a ground-floor window. It was the first time I'd seen him without his cowboy hat. He pointed at the lava demon. "You bring mighty spell?"

"Unfortunately, no. Are they going to let you out?" I asked.

He shook his head. "No say. They just ask, 'Where you from? Where you from?' Over and over. Finally, I tell them I from Gliphidetsia. They go get book. Look it up. They not going to be finding it."

There was no way they'd let him go. But I knew what to do. Hurko was close enough to the ground that he could reach us through the window. "Link hands. Transport him out of the cell." I figured they could use the same spell they'd used to move Nelda. So what if Hurko ended up in a tree? At least he'd be out of jail.

"Bad idea," Nelda said. "Hurko go through bars. Bars go through Hurko. Slice him up. We have pieces of Hurko all over."

"I destroy wall," Tortwaller said, thumping himself on the chest. "Turn bricks to water." He started to wail and roll his head from side to side.

"That spell take forever. One hour each brick," Nelda said. "Don't be such a nickel head. We grow old, you grow dizzy, hole still not big enough."

Oh man, this was definitely not good. We had to get to the school. It was almost eight. Jenna was waiting for us. I knew what Shath'dra would do—just blow away the door with a quakewave spell or hurl an ice rock at it. That was real magic. Not this useless stuff like making dust or bending silverware.

"The knife!" I said, feeling the thrill of discovering an unexpected solution. There *was* a way to get Hurko out of jail. A magical way.

27

Stopping by the Art Room for a Spell

Hurko, can you bend any kind of metal?"

He nodded. "But small like knife. Not big like bars."

"No problem. See if you can bend the bolt that's locking the door."

His face lit up. "I try."

"When you get the door open, don't run. Just walk out like there's nothing wrong. Understand?" I asked.

Hurko nodded. He crossed the cell and put his hand against the lock. Then he screamed and patted himself on top of the head. Nobody came to see what the noise was about. I guess screams were just part of the background sound in a jail. When he pushed against the cell door, it swung open. The bolt had bent enough, so it was no longer holding the door shut.

"Run!" Nelda screamed, caught up in the excitement. "Run like wind! Flee, Hurko!"

Fortunately, Hurko ignored her. He left his cell, swung the door closed behind him, and calmly disappeared from sight.

A tense moment passed before Hurko strolled out the rear exit. Zee and Nelda raced over and hugged him. "Right back soon," he said as he turned toward the building.

"Where are you going?" I asked.

"Forget hat again."

"Leave it. We have to get to the school." Carrying the lava demon, I headed to the street, with the wizards trailing along behind me. They were all bigger than I was, except for Nelda, but I couldn't help seeing myself as a duck leading a group of ducklings down a path.

"Did the police treat you okay?" I asked Hurko as we walked.

"Yes," Hurko said. "Cops good people. I work as cop."

"Back home?" I asked.

"No, back here. I watch building at night. Make sure nobody steal."

"You were a night watchman?"

"Yes. Pastor Chuck get me job. Good job. But I fall asleep one night while watchmanning. When I wake—room is full of smoke. I call nine-one-one. But I get mix up. I call one-one-nine. Nothing happen. I try over and over. Then, too late, firemen come."

I thought of all the twists of fate that had brought us to this point, starting with the fund-raiser. "Were you the watchman for Zampala Chocolates?" I asked.

"That is place," Hurko said, grinning. "Nobody steal chocolates. Not when I work. I do great job. Except one time. Still, nobody ever steal chocolates."

"Good for you," I said. Wow, if there hadn't been a fire, I wouldn't have met Hurko. For that matter, I wouldn't even have gotten to know Michelle.

By then, we'd reached the school. I took the wizards through the side entrance and down a corridor to the art room. Since the room was already crowded with statues, I left the lava demon in the hall. The lights were off, but a glow shimmered from a spot near the side wall. The kiln was on, and its door was open.

"Jenna?" I whispered as I dropped my backpack on a desk.

"Over here." She waved and I saw her dim shape at a table in a corner of the room. Two forms hovered near her. Michelle and Kyle. "Was anyone hanging around outside?" she asked when I reached her.

I shook my head. "Nope. Why?"

"Ed saw us when we walked past his house," Jenna said. "I was afraid he might wonder where we were going."

"Don't worry about it. He's on our side now. Come on, let's get started." I quickly introduced them to the wizards.

Hurko happily shook hands with everyone. Tortwaller snorted and said, "These are powerful wizards?" Nobody paid any attention to him.

Michelle turned to Zee and said, "I love your outfit."

"Thank you!" Zee said. It was the first time I'd seen her smile since we'd met.

"Strong power," Nelda said, stroking the air.

Jenna shot me a grin. "I told you it was me they felt."

If that made her happy, I wasn't going to argue. Even if she was completely wrong. "Is everything ready?" I asked.

"It's all set." Jenna lifted a bowl from the table. Something very smelly sloshed inside.

"Are you sure about this?" I asked.

"Positive," Jenna said. "Wait, I almost forgot." She put the bowl down and grabbed a pair of scissors. "I need a lock of hair. That'll help make sure the portal leads to where you came from."

Nelda stepped forward and let Jenna snip a bit of her hair. Jenna sprinkled the clippings over the mixture, then carried the bowl to the kiln. Kyle grabbed a book from the table and followed her.

"Are you *absolutely* sure?" I asked.

"Yes, I am, Mercer. They'll go back where they came from. Okay? Clear enough? Could you please stop questioning everything I do?"

"Sure. Sorry."

Jenna nodded to Kyle, who held the book where she could see it. "Everyone, repeat what I say," she told us.

I moved behind the wizards. Heat washed across my face and the light threw weird shadows against the wall. I looked over at Michelle. She looked back at me, her face unsure but achingly pretty in the electric glow of the kiln.

"Portal of the many worlds," Jenna said, reading from the book.

Feeling halfway silly and halfway scared, I repeated the chant along with everyone else.

Jenna dipped the fingers of her left hand into the bowl and flicked a spray of drops toward the kiln. A bright flash flared up, then died. The air smelled like burned toast.

"Find the way the wayward seek . . ."

We repeated it. Jenna fed the flames again.

"Portal of the many worlds . . ."

Another bright flash. *Many worlds.* As I heard those words, I thought about the other worlds the wizards had seen on their way here. A world of ice. A world of monsters. Were we about to roll the dice?

"Open now and span the void."

Jenna shoved her hands forward, tossing the contents of the bowl into the kiln. There was one heck of a whoosh, so bright it left a floating spot of light in my eyes, like when Dad used the flash on his camera.

Michelle was the first one to gasp. It took me a second longer than her to realize what was happening. When I did, I gasped, too. The spot of light wasn't an afterimage. It was real. And it was growing larger. Larger and brighter.

Jenna had opened a portal.

28

Mind If I Cut In?

The next three things happened pretty much at once.

First, Jenna pointed at the portal, which had already grown large enough to enter, and told the wizards, "Step right in. It will take you back."

Second, Ed dashed into the room. "I *knew* you guys were playing here at night. I finally figured out how to get past that boulder. Can I join—" He froze in midsentence as his eyes scanned the scene. Then he pointed at the portal and said, "What in the world is *that*?"

The third thing actually climbed out of the portal.

An arm emerged first, as if feeling the way.

"What is it?" Michelle whispered when the head came through.

I took a step away from the portal. "Oh man, Jenna. I think you opened up the wrong door." This wouldn't send the wizards to their world. It would send them to the last world they'd seen—the world of the monsters who'd left their mark on Hurko. Worse, it gave the monsters a way to reach our world.

The creature's face, hard and dry like an old plaster cast, with black diamonds for eyes, turned toward me as the rest of the body emerged from the portal. Long arms, jointed like insect legs, probed the air. I gazed up at the creature as it rose to its full height. If a mummy had married a praying mantis, this is what their children would have looked like.

The creature stepped forward, its feet scraping across the floor with a sound that made my spine shiver. Beams of red light laced back and forth between its body and the portal, pulsing like arteries. Behind the portal, the glow from the kiln faded. The liquid had shorted something. But the portal existed on its own now, without any need of the kiln.

"We come in peace," Jenna said, which struck me as an amazingly stupid statement, since we weren't the ones who had come.

Kyle dropped the book to the floor. Ed made a gulping sound, like he was trying to swallow a baseball.

"Stay calm," I said. "We outnumber him. We'll be fine."

The creature howled and flung his arms wide. Small fireballs shot from his fingertips like a spray of bullets. I ducked, but the missiles weren't aimed at us. Instead, they fanned out. Most of them struck the statues spread through the room. A handful flew out the door with a whoosh.

The statues glowed as if lit from within. Then they moved. All around us, the monsters of Zule awakened. They crept forward, their weapons raised, their claws spread. I turned toward the door, but it was blocked by my lava demon, who'd lurched in from the hallway. All we made was bad guys, I realized. No heroes. No help. We'd filled the room with enemies who'd attack a player—or a kid—on sight.

Ed yelped and scurried away from the door, joining us midway between the lava demon and the creature from the portal.

It's only papier-mâché, I thought. Just newspapers and paste. *I made you. And I can destroy you.* I charged at the demon, hoping to ram it with my shoulder and knock it over.

It flicked out an arm the instant I was in range. The blow sent me tumbling to the floor. I felt like I'd been kicked by a horse. Maybe a horse riding on a freight train. The lava demon was no longer just newspaper and paste. There was bad magic happening here. I gasped, forcing air back into my lungs. The demon smashed his fist down on a table, shattering it. Then he moved toward me.

Behind the demon, in the hallway, I saw a shadowy figure. As he came closer, the light from the portal revealed Donny.

"Run!" I yelled. "Get out of here." At least he'd be able to escape and call for help. But I was afraid it would all be over before help arrived.

Donny raised his mop in his left hand. He slashed at it with his right, shearing off the end. The mop head went flying. Donny stepped through the door, gripping the stick with two hands like a martial arts master. He rushed at the lava demon, swinging the stick so fast, I couldn't even see the motion. I heard three loud whacks. With each strike, a flash of green light burst from the impact area. A fourth strike, more powerful than the others, crushed the lava demon's head. The statue crumpled to the floor. But there was still a roomful of other statues to deal with.

Donny jumped over the fallen monster and faced the creature from the portal. Roaring a cry of rage, the creature thrust both hands toward Donny, sending out a huge fireball.

I flinched. But Donny knocked the fireball aside with the stick. It hit the wall and dissolved in a shower of sparks. Then he slashed the stick to his left, taking out another of the statues. "I could use some help," he said.

"What should we do?" I asked.

"Whatever you can," he said as he deflected two more fireballs. He nodded toward the wizards. "Get them to help fight. You can handle the smaller ones."

"Hurko!" I shouted, pointing at a rock-python that was slithering toward him.

He grabbed a chair and swung it at the monster. The chair broke, but the rock-python stopped, as if stunned by the blow. The other wizards joined in. I heard Nelda's cry of "Stupid statue" every time she hit something.

Donny glanced toward Ed, who had backed up near the windows. "You, pray."

"Pray?" Ed asked. "In school? I could get in trouble for that."

"Shut up and pray," Donny said. "We need all the help we can get."

Ed dropped to his knees.

I punched at an ice demon and nearly broke my fist. In a game, I'd never have made that mistake. As I scanned the room in search of a weapon, I saw Jenna hit a troll with a flying kick. The statue went down, but so did Jenna. She tried to stand, then grabbed her knee and dropped to the floor.

Michelle was swinging an easel like a field hockey stick. She hit one of the ogres, knocking it back, but the easel splintered in her hands.

To my right, Kyle was wrestling with a centaur. As I raced over to help him, sharp claws dug into my shoulders and tried to drag me to the floor. I spun hard, ripping my shirt when I twisted free, and found myself face-to-face with a skull demon.

Across the room, the creature from the portal howled in triumph as a fireball struck Donny on the left arm. He staggered back, nearly dropping his weapon. His overalls smoldered and his face showed a mix of pain and exhaustion.

We were losing. And this was no game.

29

Dust in the Nick of Time

Before I could get away, the skull demon clutched my throat and tried to force me to the floor. He squeezed my neck so hard, the room began to fade. Through the dying light, I saw something move at my feet. It was Shath'dra. The tiny figure had come to life, too. He must have cut his way out of my backpack. He raised his sword and plunged it into the foot of the skull demon.

The miniature attack wasn't enough to free me. The demon still held on as he glanced at his foot. Odds are he wouldn't be distracted for more than an instant. Maybe that would be enough. I was so dizzy now, I knew I'd only get one chance to break free. I grabbed his wrists, but I didn't try to yank them from my throat. Instead, I stepped backward and pulled at the demon, then turned to the side, hoping to catch him off balance and fling him the way Jenna had thrown me the other day.

It worked. Sort of. We staggered. The demon spun past me, still holding my throat, but I could feel his grip slipping. Shath'dra went flying across the room as the demon's foot whipped through the air. He hit the bulletin board sword-first and stuck there.

I gathered my strength for one more move. Using the demon's momentum as we swung around, I pushed him. Hard. He let go and tumbled into the red beams of light that tied the creature to the portal.

The instant the skull demon touched the beams, he exploded like he'd been stuffed with gunpowder. Suddenly, I was pushing against nothing but air. In back of me, I heard the creature from the portal cry out. Donny must have landed a blow. But there was no time to look. As a shower of papier-mâché struck my face, I fell forward toward the beams. My hands shot out, but there was nothing to grab— no way to stop from toppling into the deadly red light.

Strong hands locked on to my arm and pulled me back to safety. Hurko's hands. Before I could thank him, a tree sprite charged at us. Thankfully, it was one of the smaller statues. Hurko and I lifted it from the ground and tossed it into the beams. As I turned away from the explosion, I saw the creature from the portal stagger for an instant, allowing Donny to land another strike. And I suddenly realized the connection.

"We have to block the beams," I said to Hurko. "The light from the portal gives the creature its power." I grabbed a drawing pad from a table and pushed it into the pulsing red lights. A jolt of fire shot through my hands as the pad exploded. I felt like I'd just plunged my fingers in a vat of acid. The creature staggered again, but so briefly that Donny couldn't take advantage of the opening.

Above the sound of battle that filled the room, I heard noise in the hallway. Maybe help was coming. I ran over and looked out the door. And my heart stopped.

I'd forgotten about the statues in the gym. They were coming to join the fight. Ogres and trolls and demons. More statues spilled from the cafeteria, blocking any chance we had of escaping down the other end of the hall. We were about to become badly outnumbered.

I checked the room. Jenna was hurt. Michelle was jabbing at one enemy with a piece of wood from the easel, but another was crawling toward her. She wouldn't be able to fight them off for long. Kyle was still locked in battle with the centaur. The wizards were struggling against the smaller statues. Shath'dra, who'd freed himself from the bulletin board, was hacking away at the rear leg of a fire wolf. I figured he'd have it hobbled in about twenty minutes. Nelda, clutching a chalkboard eraser in one hand, looked like she was trying to cast a spell, but what was the use? None of their spells could do any good. Talking animals wouldn't help us here. Or bent metal. And we had no use for—

That was it! "Tortwaller," I called, holding out my hands. "Do your dust spell. And keep doing it." I hoped he understood my plan. There was no time to explain. And I hoped he wasn't limited to casting the spell on sneakers.

He pushed back the demon he was fighting and did his magic. My hands tickled with the oddest feeling, as if my skin were trying to crawl away. Dust appeared on my palms. A fine layer, first, then more and more, growing thicker until I could feel the weight of it.

I raised my hands and blew hard, sending the dust toward the deadly beams that linked the creature to the portal. As I emptied the last breath from my lungs, I thought about the other time, days ago, when I'd seen a cloud of flour dust block the sunlight in this same room.

The dust met the beams, hissing and snapping like a billion miniature firecrackers, filling the air with the odor of burning hair. But it worked—the beams dimmed and the creature slowed.

Donny leaped forward and slashed his weapon, raining blows on the creature. It staggered backward, raising its arms against the assault.

"Zee!" I called. "Your turn. Do your magic." I grabbed the basket from Ms. MacIntosh's desk and hurled the apples toward the creature.

Zee cast her spell, liquefying the tumbling fruit and turning the floor at the creature's feet to a slimy, slippery muck. One of its feet slipped, and the creature staggered.

Donny thrust out his stick, jabbing his target dead center in the chest. With a hard push, he sent the creature sliding toward the portal.

The creature fell halfway into the glowing doorway. Donny stepped forward to deliver a final strike, but he slipped on the floor, too.

He tried to rise, but it wasn't necessary. A chalkboard eraser shot across the room and smacked the creature in the forehead.

"Stupid monster," Nelda said as she dusted her hands.

The instant the creature tumbled back into its world, Donny, still on his knees, dropped the stick, waved his hands in an intricate pattern, and spoke words in a language I'd never heard before.

The portal disappeared with a whoosh.

30

Mopping Up

Around us, the statues froze. Some, caught in midstep, toppled over. A couple rocked in place, like tottering bowling pins. But they were all lifeless papier-mâché again. Or lifeless metal. I saw Shath'dra on the floor, his sword frozen in midslash. I picked him up. "At least we got to fight side by side for a little while," I said. Then I put him in my pocket.

"Everybody okay?" Donny asked, flipping on the light.

I checked around the room. Jenna, back on her feet, leaned against a table. Kyle was pulling his arms and legs free from the centaur. Michelle seemed unhurt. So did the wizards. Ed was still on his knees, his face as pale as flour paste.

"You're not just a janitor," I said to Donny. "Are you?"

He shrugged. "You think one person could keep this

whole place clean without a little magic? Speaking of which . . ." He walked over to Jenna's book and jabbed it with his stick. There was a small bang and the book turned to ashes. "No more spells for you, young lady. Okay?"

"Okay," Jenna said. I'd never seen her look sheepish before.

Others in the room were not so quiet.

"Magus!" Hurko cried.

"Magus!" the other wizards cried. They dropped to their knees.

"Are you from their world?" I asked.

Donny shook his head. "No. But I can help them go back."

"So where are you from?" I asked.

"A place very much like Zule," he said. "With wizards trained for combat and warriors schooled in sorcery."

"Wow. That must be awesome," I said, my pulse quickening at the thought.

Donny didn't answer me. Instead, he looked around the room. I followed his gaze to the scattered statues, lying like broken corpses on a battlefield. In my mind, I saw what it would be like if they were flesh and blood rather than paper and paste. My stomach churned at the thought of real swords slicing through real bodies.

At that moment, I understood why Donny had chosen to spend his days mopping floors and chatting with eighth graders. I also knew I'd be happy to stick with fantasy games from now on. No more real-life spells.

"You kids, step outside," Donny said.

I realized he was going to send the wizards home right now. I went to Hurko and held out my hand. He stepped forward and gave me a hug, almost breaking my ribs.

"Magus," he whispered.

"Magus," I said back to him.

I said good-bye to the others, getting hugs from all of them—even Tortwaller. "You're very powerful," I told him.

"You are clever," he told me. "For someone who does not know spells."

Kyle, Jenna, Ed, Michelle, and I left the room and closed the door. There were no explosions or flashes of light, but a moment later, somehow, I knew the wizards were gone.

Right after that, Donny came out. Alone. He looked exhausted. "Silence?" he asked.

I nodded. "We'll never tell."

He stared at me for a moment, then nodded back. I knew he'd decided he could trust us with his secret. "And no more fooling around with sorcery," he said.

"Don't worry. I'm sticking with games," I said.

"It wasn't you who opened the portal, Mercer," Jenna said. "It was me." She looked at Donny. "I did it, right?"

He shook his head. "Nobody born of this world has the power for sorcery," he said.

"Then how'd the portal open?" I asked.

"From the other side," he said. "You had four wizards trying to cast the spell, and a fifth just down the hallway. Not enough to open a portal, but enough to send a signal to that creature's world. It's like you flipped on your porch light on a dark night. They found you, and five of them created the portal from their side. It's a good thing just one of them came through."

"So the power that Nelda felt all through the town was yours," I said.

Donny nodded.

I sighed. "For a while, I thought I could really do magic."

"There's more than one kind of magic," Donny said. "Each universe has its own. When you play your games, when you create a world in your head, that's magic." He glanced at Ed. "And when you write, that's magic."

Ed didn't answer. He looked like he was in shock.

Donny walked over to him. "Don't question your faith," he said. "What happened here is about other worlds, not your world. Do you understand?"

"I guess," Ed said.

Donny patted him on the shoulder. "Go home, now. All of you. I have a lot of cleaning up to do." He glanced over his shoulder at the art room.

"Thanks," I said to Donny.

As we left the school, I kept expecting someone to say

something. But we were all quiet. I guess each of us was trying to fit what we'd seen into our view of the universe. I wondered whether it would be hardest for Ed. Maybe not. Maybe it would be easiest, because he knew what he believed. For the first time, I envied him.

31

Fun and No Games

The fund-raiser was a big success. How could it fail, when we'd combined a fashion show and a garage sale with an international street fair? Basically, we'd ended up back at the start, using Ed's and Michelle's original ideas. All that was missing was the part I'd wanted. We had no fantasy games. No tournament. No convention. But that wasn't important right now. At the end of the day, as Michelle and I handed the money to Pastor Chuck, I felt proud of what we'd accomplished. Because of us, hungry people would be fed.

"Thank you," Pastor Chuck said. "This will be put to very good use. I can promise you that. I hope you aren't going to disappear now that the fund-raiser's over. You're still planning to stop by once in a while, aren't you?"

"Sure," I said. "How could I stay away? I have this irresistible craving for Chuck steak."

"We promise we'll visit whenever we can," Michelle said.

"Maybe you can buy a dishwasher now," I said.

"No need. I've already got a great one." Pastor Chuck thanked us again and left.

"Sorry you didn't get to run your tournament," Michelle said.

"That's okay. At least we can play in school again." We'd gotten permission, thanks to another column Ed wrote for *The Wilde Times*. His headline was "The Magic Power of Imagination." Fortunately, this one wasn't exciting enough for the *Cryer*, so no outsiders read it.

Kyle waved at us on his way out. "Good job," he said. "See you Monday."

"See you." I looked around the gym. The last of the crowd was leaving. Over by the bleachers, Ed and Jenna were folding up tables together and arguing about something. I got the impression they were each trying to convert the other.

Our experience had brought us all closer together. I think I understood Ed a lot better now. And I could talk to Michelle without feeling like a complete idiot. That alone made it worth facing a roomful of demons.

"I've been designing my own game," I told her. The players took the role of wizards stuck in a world without magic. They did best if they worked together. Their spells didn't seem powerful. But they were, if used the right way. "Want to hear about it?"

Michelle smiled. "I'd like that."

As we walked across the gym toward the exit, I spotted Donny, who was already starting to sweep the floor. He saw me watching and smiled. Donny the janitor—now there was a real hero.

"Magus," I said. I spoke softly, to myself, but I had the feeling he heard.